Last Voyage a the *Vengeferth*

G. A. Schindler

copyright © 2017 G. A. Schindler

first edition

edited by Doc Fisher

and Kathy Joyce

cover design by G. A. Schindler

All rights reserved.
ISBN-13:978-1542569712
ISBN-10:1542569710

CONTENTS

	Thanks	5
I	Aboard the *Vengeferth*	8
II	Aboard the smallboat	49
III	Aboard the *Crazy Cousin*	89
	You're charged	127

A big thank you to the world's best wife, Susie, who in countless ways made this book possible. She's the best good thing that ever happened to me.

Her Voice

When I first heard her
Voice blew through me
Like wind through a whistle.
She hit me
Rolling eighteen wheeler fast
And I was road pizza.

I also thank the Sterling Heights writing group. This tome wouldn't have begun, nor improved to its current state but for your assistance.

An' thanks much to my best friends Captain an' Doc, who oft assisted my recollections. Especially to patient Doc, for making time to edit.

This story begs a moderate reading pace foreign to today's high speed world. Ya may experience it like swimming a late spring river, tensed up upon diving in, till you relax an' enjoy merging with the flow.

Last Voyage a the *Vengeferth*

Aye, I'm Wil DeVoe. I sailed as first mate aboard the *Vengeferth*. Amid our last trip out, the far known Captain Werthman charged me with someday putting ta the page a clear record a the events a that wondrous adventure. Now I found the someday, an' this page appears ready ta take on the voyage's clearest account my hand can pen.

First, my apology ta ya men readers who put down your tuppence for this tome. Apology's for leaving out the hard language ya might prefer left in. Aye, 'twas there, salty sprinkled through, as where'er seafaring men are found. But I swear the tale can be well told without it. ('Tis humor, *swearing* not ta use the *swearing* words.) I must leave out the hard language, or apologize ta the ladies an' youngsters on its account.

Aye, I'll leave out much a the more humdrum, *trying* stuff as well. Stuff *trying* a body's patience an' *trying* ta lower eyelids inta sleep. Yet rest assured our trip held far enough tribulations ta fill a hefty tome. I'll go ta the grave recalling it frightfully clear. I swear I'm about ta use this fine feather pen's blackest ink ta stow ya aboard an' send ya smelling salty breezes an' pickle brine on the *Last Voyage a the Vengeferth*.

(I) Aboard the *Vengeferth*

(1) The white

'Twas done 'fore the boy knew. 'Fore any crewman knew. The beast charged straight up from the black bowels a hell an' swirled back unseen. Though the white didn't show himself, the water's fierce roiling told the experienced eye he was of no modest size. We stood helpless and stunned witless. Best good thing was the quickness. The boy never knew it happened.

He'd done the smart thing. The boy'd listened well when I told 'im if he struggled they'd tie 'im ta the chair, an' it could go worse. He sat right down on it, an' stayed under a time, 'fore climbing up ta poke his head out gasping. But then the brute hit. He *should* a been okay. I s*wear* I didn't mean ta *lie* ta the boy. There's no knowing about whites. Just no knowing.

We began ta haul up the chair, but Captain wouldn't have it. He cut the line. His grim face white as the mainsail. Had ta be angered at 'imself for giving o'er ta such foolishness, an' perhaps already with a touch a fear. His mouth was a thin line, an' his eyes clenched 'til ya thought 'em closed.

Aloose, the chair took a notion ta float. Ten feet out it hung in a red pool. It sat still, an' we stared. Seemed near an hour. Till, just as sudden, it tipped an' sunk, sucking the line down like a last noodle.

We'd had our time a prayer. Praying was o'er, an' Captain strode ta his cabin, eyes narrow ahead, saying nothing an' seeing nobody. We cleared his path more with fear than respect. There was little respect ta be found for 'im about then.

Later he came ta mess. We'd a gone silent if we weren't already. Usual chat wasn't in us. Spoons clicking on plates sounded loud, till that too stopped when he showed his face.

"Men, ya know the boy wasn't meant ta die," Captain offered low, eyes down, a tremble in his voice as though speaking ta God. "He was a feisty sort, an' certainly didn't deserve it. Too sadly, what's done's done. Can't bring 'im back."

Captain's o'er-sized nose was red.

"Thing I can find ta do is seek out revenge on the ugly brute that took 'im," Captain's voice came up stronger. "When they get a good meal, ya know they don't always hurry off. More oft they hang about expecting another morsel. Jack, sharpen the old harpoons tonight. 'Tis a fearfull mean business an' mine alone. I'll ask no man ta join me, though a volunteer or two wouldn't be turned away. Cookie, pull the two toughest steaks from the larder. Sorry ta give the beast one a our meals, boys. We'll get us some better meat from next ship we take."

Good luck ta Cookie sorting that out. Seems ta me shoe leather's all shoe leather by any name. As for Captain Werthman, I was thinking he aimed ta gain back respect, an' he might have worries about the boy's ghost. We've all heard enough stories about spirits an' such ta feel there might be a string a truth in 'em. Some believe stronger 'n others. Never heard Captain's take on that, but wasting a day ridding the sea a the white, seemed at least partly meant ta beg mercy from the boy's spirit should it e'er show.

There was little talk that eve. Boy's loss'd sunk our spirits. 'Twas sweaty warm. The water lay with a calmness seamen enjoy describing as being smooth as your sweet lass's cheek.

Smallboats aren't the least like whaling boats, but the Captain had one rigged as close as he could. 'Twas too small by half an' the wrong shape. Mostly 'twasn't deep enough. Captain's craft had ta be an easy tip. Coil a cord in the middle being too high. We had little true whaling line. His was too heavy. Whaling line's near as strong but lighter an' less thick. Being as he was out for shark an' not whale, the smallboat seemed likely ta do well enough if she didn't tip. I could see no real need for Captain Werthman ta tie on all that line. Yet he owned a burning desire ta have certainty the beast was done.

He'd no gun ta shoot the harpoons. The boat wasn't big enough for a harpoon gun. Kickback'd be a sure tip. Captain had three old wooden handled ones ta heave. He'd long had 'em stowed. Five foot a true whaling line tied one on ta the top a the coil. I wondered about the bother a having three harpoons. No chance y'd have time ta retie a second one ta the line. But our grim eyed Captain had 'im some idea.

Morn brought the slightest breeze. There was little chop when we winched the three down the side. Our tall Captain with his salt-an'-pepper beard, large nose, an' wide brim, wasn't alone in the smallboat. Aiming ta impress, youthfull Willie B an' Jonesy were along. Those muscular adventurers climbed too easily aboard. Their smooth faces didn't wear the seriousness a the situation. They lacked scare in their eyes.

"Worst ya can do is step in the coil, boys," Captain advised as we lowered the three in that too small boat.

A cool breeze was picking up, an' clouds were moving in.

(2) The fight

Going for shark begs no imagination. Ya fling your bloody bait out there an' ya wait. Captain's steaks were but ten foot out. Too near for my liking. A course ya couldn't heave them heavy harpoons far, so I guess he needed his bait too close.

'Twas was the picture. Our grim Captain standing ta the fore, Willie B an' Jonesy seated aft. The three near twenty foot out in that too small boat, with a coil a line piled high in the middle an' the bait but ten foot out from them. The crew was scattered in the riggin, our squinting eyes searching for a shark shadow. 'Twas some hour a waiting. No little sharks nibbling about seemed ta say there was a big one near, scaring 'em off. They usually come in slow, at the surface, their fin cutting waves like Captain's dagger. From up in the riggin, most are shadows easy ta spot. Not the whites. They're not really white but pale enough ta be hard ta see. Especially if they come in too deep for their scary big fin ta cut waves.

This monster surprised 'cause she again came from under. Right from the bottom, like charging from the devil's deepest pit a hell. She was scary big. Surely the biggest I ever saw. An' this time jumping half a body up from the water. Could a told her the steaks were tough an' not worth near the effort. But 'twasn't me had the brute's ear. 'Twas the devil 'imself.

Up shadowing o'er that tiny boat she went. If the beast fell their way, the three'd be her supper for sure. Easy pickins. But she went sideways from 'em, an' Captain thrust the harpoon inta her side as she began down.

Now, the side's not the best place ta hit 'em. About the same as the back. They just swim 'round a bit, shake your harpoon aloose, an' have but another scar for your trouble. If ya hit one like that, about the only chance the brute's finished is if she's slowed an' bleeding enough so's her friends feed on her.

This one took the harpoon an' headed straight out. White smoke an' shrillest whine filled the air, line sawing the smallboat's rail as it reeled out. We held breaths up top, asking in our heads what'd happen when a line on something that huge ran out. Many prayed. The bottom end a the coil was tied on ta the smallboat. A line tied on the smallboat ta the ship.

Right off, Willie B jumps in an' swims toward us. He's going near as fast's the beast. We drop a line, an' he scrambles wide eyed up the side. Just then the white turns sideways an' stops. We see her treading water, seeming ta wait on something. Much a the coil was gone from the boat's floor, an' the line was slack. 'Twas a scared silence. All awaited what was next.

Jonesy'd espied Willie clambering o'er the rail an' saw his pal'd done the smart thing. So he decided ta come unfroze an' follow. But in his hurry, Jonesy stepped in the coil. 'Twas meant as a quick step on his way ta dive toward the ship. But as though the espying devil 'imself whispered in her ear, the best yanked e**xact**ly then!

Jonesy's head smacked the smallboat rail loud like a cannon. Had ta be dead 'fore he hit the water. The line about his ankle spun 'im a quick turn an' set 'im aloose ta float twenty foot out.

Musta been Jonesy's head booming the rail that turned the beast sideways again with maybe ten foot a line left in the coil. Not two seconds passed till we saw the smell a Jonesy's blood pull the monster back fast as she'd been running out.

"She's a coming back for Jonesy, Captain!" Evans screech came from high in the riggin.

Our tall Captain was ghosty white an' fiercely atremble. He'd no need ta jump in the water an' swim for it. Any time he could grab the line ta the ship an' pull his perilous self near enough ta catch a tossed line. It wouldn't take a half minute. He stood stiff, awaiting the onrushing beast, his white knuckles glued ta the second harpoon, its hilt tucked 'neath his arm.

Well, our Captain Werthman got as fortunate as any man in such a poor situation can imagine. The white slowed some as she came cutting in. She hit Jonesy, an' carried his sideways body up nearly ta the Captain's lap. He reflexed for'd, thrusting the harpoon through the shark's left eye directly ta her small brain. The brute's last twitch was backwards. Captain clung ta the harpoon. She flung 'im high an' near thirty foot out. The harpoon stayed with the white. Its wood handle was the last thing ta disappear as the beast's dead weight sunk back. She took Jonesy along, down inta the black depths.

(3) Gorden shows 'imself

We quick jumped in the smallboat ta go fetch the Captain. He was thrashing about unhurt, but might a had ta shuck clothes ta swim if he didn't see us coming.

Climbing up the line, he barked back o'er his shoulder, "Use that last harpoon ta cut the cursed beast aloose."

"Can't afford the cordage, Captain," Gorden answered clear.

All went quiet. Captain turned ta see who'd spoke. Ya could be in trouble crossing 'im on the rare occasion his mood was bad. His mood couldn't a been worse. Gorden's words would a been better spoke as a question, but all heard the truth simply put. We'd lost line with the chair, an' that cordage hanging ta the shark was more 'n any man should waste. Any seaman knew ships could be lost ta squalls for lack a line.

"Right, Mr. Gorden," Captain growled. "Yet leave the bitter end down a time so's it comes up clean." He turned, stepped o'er the rail, an' strode ta his quarters.

Mess was quiet again that eve. Cookie spiced up the stew a

tad meaning ta improve appetites, but it didn't work. The crew sat digesting more 'n the food. Lotsa ways ya might look at the goings on a the last two days. I could see in their eyes, the men were mulling it 'round in their minds.

    Anger was easy ta be had. At the Captain for sending the boy under, so youthfull an' undeserving. An' for losing Jonesy too. Ta be fair, we heard 'im warned on the danger a stepping in the coil. Yet our spirits were lowered by his loss. He wasn't the smartest nor most cheerfull amongst us, but he'd had a strong back an' was a good fighter ta stand by your side. 'Twas yet ta be seen when his pal, Willie B'd come ta his senses. For all purposes, we'd be short a second good man for a time.

    Yet bravery was there ta be seen. No matter how foolish ya might take it, going after the white, an' standing with the shakes awaiting the beast, spoke a the Captain's bravery. An' none'd deny ridding the sea a that ugly brute was a good thing.

    Mostly I found foolishness in it. Putting the boy, guilty a nothing, in such a bad situation was hard ta fathom. It spoke poorly on the workings a the Captain's mind. An' wanting ta cut the line an' be rid a all trace was understandable, yet the foolishness a wasting so much line was plain ta see.

    Mayhap the Captain's bravery an' skill at taking down such a beast outweighed all in the men's minds. I'd listen ta idle chatter an' gently sound out the men ta measure their take on it. He might be asking me about it.

    The one good ta come out a that two day muddle was finding the crew's leader. Gorden had shown 'imself. A crew needs a leader. We were twelve days out an' 'twas about time. Captain'd name a steward if he must, but having one name 'imself was far the better. Some'd fight for the job first day out, others came on it reluctant. The best fall betwixt--willing but not so anxious. Gorden seemed solid on that account.

    I had ta get ta know 'im. 'Twas me, first mate, who'd work with 'im. He'd be the one the men jawed with, I was the first mate he'd jaw with, an' I'd jaw with Captain Werthman. 'Tis how 'twent. Uncomplicated. Simple an' straight.

There were no fancy titles aboard the *Vengeferth*. Doc an' Cookie, each with a helper. In a battle, Doc'd stay below an' Cookie on deck. Others went o'er the side. Each crewman had specialties an' day ta day duties, but no fancy titles or nothing.

The *Vengeferth* wasn't big. Traded her size for speed. Built wide atop, but narrow below, she'd outrun an' outmaneuver most any vessel afloat. But her size meant tight quarters for a crew about forty strong. An', aboard her, squalls could be most frightfull. The fiercest could age a new man o'ernight. Cannons had ta be smaller too. Kickback a big ones could tip a small ship or tear it asunder. I've heard more 'n one Captain's rolled his own ship taking aboard an' firing cannons too big.

No, our *Vengeferth* wasn't a sizable vessel, but our foxy Captain Werthman had more 'n speed up his sleeve. He brought ta the fray six cannons that threw strangely shaped lethal balls, the likes a which none had seen. A spyglass, excellent beyond imagination, was kept on the quarter deck as well. Captain heard about it in the east. His uncle, first mate on a frigate, brought it 'round the Cape a Good Hope for 'im.

Our speed, amazing spyglass, an' deadly cannons, far made up for our *Vengeferth's* lack a size. That glass, if watched close on the quarterdeck, gave us the advantage a seeing any ship's jib 'fore they spotted us. Then, somehow through that glass, the Captain'd fathom a most exact distance ta far ships, so's we could take out their main mast with his deadly accurate, funny shaped cannon balls. More 'n that, the amazing cannons could do it in a fair chop, if the wind was steady. Small ships rolled in heavy seas such that cannons were useless. Couldn't be aimed. Not so on our *Vengeferth*. Had ta get some closer in high chop, but somehow Captain's dead accuracy was there.

(4) "Some plans go awry."

After the morn's craziness, I checked that Cookie's help, Tom, was getting the men noon mess, bread an' cheese, late though 'twas. I saw the men were back ta busy, an' went below ta rest an' read till eve mess. I was no spring chick. O'er twice the age a most aboard--past a half century. In emergency times I kept up, but it wore on me. Needed my rest.

Seeing about Gorden was my day's chore. 'Fore late mess I stepped for'rd ta the Captain's quarters an' knocked. He called me in upon identifying myself. The door wasn't its usual locked. Found 'im abed, damp clothing still on. A foundering candle left the room dingy, an' noon mess sat cold on his desk.

"Captain Werthman, ya gotta get out a those clothes an' in a warm shower, else ya take sick," I urged. We bathed less seldom on the *Vengeferth* than most ships. Sea water was pumped ta a tank atop a tiny water closet. Salt water's not the best for bathing, an' the soap was poor. 'Twas nearer punishment than treat. We'd add hot water from the galley on rare times.

"The boy wasn't ta' die, Wil," He choked, facing the wall.

"A course not, Captain. Yet, like ya declared, what's done's done. He can't be fetched back. Sending the beast down was what ya could do, an' getting yourself sick won't help."

"Sending that white down did nothing," He spat. "I deserve all the illness it takes ta kill me slow an' well tortured."

"Don't talk like that, Captain. Our Lord knows intentions."

"'Twas more his initiation than punishment for sneaking aboard, Wil. He was ta come up with a tad more growth."

"Some plans go awry, Captain. Nothing more ta be said. Ya must explain the intent ta the crew. With 'em understanding it, an' ya putting down the shark, I know they'll be behind ya."

"I'm undeserving a anyone behind me, Wil. I doubt that poor boy'd be behind me."

"It's no matter, Captain. 'Tis what's right. I'll get men ta' pump up water for a shower, an' have 'em fetch hot from the galley ta heat it. Here's a cover o'er ya. Wait ta climb out an' shuck those clothes till we get the warm shower ready."

Now I saw Captain's mind an' it made sense. We'd never had a stowaway. Boy hid aboard ta be a pirate. Had ta be tested, much for his own sake. Captain *did* right. All just went awry.

I was eased that he didn't carry on about fearsome spirits an' such. Ta my mind, 'tis the worry a scares that calls 'em 'round.

They can be a man's ruination. I've not seen it, praise the Lord, but heard it told more 'n once by sober, solid witnesses.

I got the Captain showered an' eating. He'd set Gorden's folder on his desk by the food tray. Things settled down, so I took the folder ta my room ta learn what I could.

There was little ta glean from Jamie R. Gorden's folder. Few a the men's folders held much. He'd been a smith. Put his sister Rosie's address, ta notify. His name, hers, an' her address written in his own good hand, showed he could use pen an' paper. Gave his age a twenty two. Made 'im older 'n half the crew. Oldsters are few aboard pirate ships. I had fifteen years on our crew's eldest, ten on the Captain. I take it back. Doc had six years on the Captain, though he didn't look it. Cookie was a few years younger, behind a big beard hiding his even bigger belly.

As for Gorden taking on the crew's lead, likely he'd measure up, though this being but his second trip might sway it against 'im. An' he wore the long girlie hair some a the younger bucks favored. Girls ashore seemed ta fancy it, though me 'n the Captain didn't. I'd soon tell 'im he couldn't take it ta the riggin aloose. If a crewman's hair tangles in the lines, he's is a gonner.

Gorden'd been a good learner with the sword though. Took it serious an' went at it long hours. Amid last trip he'd been putting mean welts on good men. By trips end, he was off the wood practice sword an' working against the best. Yet ya had ta be carefull. Corked tips an' covered edges were uncertain. Ships lost good man ta sword practice. In my days, I've twice seen the price a mistakes be dearly high, as both times it happened amongst the nearest a friends.

Gorden couldn't yet work the riggin. Hadn't put in the time. Some years a smithing, followed by hours on deck with the sword, gave his body a fine cut. He showed nimble afoot, an' promised ta do fine atop when he gave the time. 'Twas good ta see he could put pen ta paper as well. I searched 'im out in the crew's quarters, an' asked 'im up ta the quarter deck.

(5) Recruiting Gorden

We settled in, side by side, leaning elbows on the rail. Water lay flat 'fore the waning sun. Dusk was oft a still time, but felt a deeper quiet in the wake a such turmoil. He offered lowly, "Worrysome time, Mister DeVoe," sounding older 'n his years.

"No doubt, no doubt," I nodded. "An ugly bad start for a trip. Bound ta settle down though."

"Sure hope so," He sighed, facing out ta sea.

I had an extra pipe an' offered it as I put tobacco in mine.

"Thanks, Mister DeVoe, but I don't take pleasure in smoke. Not that I care that others do. I enjoy the smell at a distance. My dad didn't touch it though. He heard old smokers coughing an' wheezing, an' held the firm belief tobacco was the farthest thing from healthfull. I'm less sure on it, but I know he was purely a wise man. I've not found fault with any a his ideas yet, an' till I do, I expect I'll avoid the tobacco."

"Smart ta bide by your dad's wisdom, Mr. Gorden. Too many young blokes hurry ta go against a father's every word," I nodded, well glad ta turn our talk from recent goings on.

"Oh I might a done the rebelling, were he the heavy handed sort. But he always explained his logic in an easy way, an' then let me go my own direction. I could never find fault in his logic, so going another way never made sense. He passed a year 'fore I joined the crew. I'm not so sure he'd agree with me throwing in with pirates."

"Mayhap not," I nodded an' puffed. Our belts ta the rail, his chiseled face lit orange by the sun fast sinking. "Sounds like a good man. Sorry ta hear ya lost 'im. How'd it happen?"

"Carrying a heavy sack on his shoulder, he misstepped an' fell ta the street. Run o'er by horse an' wagon. Most sad an' ugly for us, but surely nobody's fault."

"Sounds mercyfull quick at least, as we all wish when 'tis our time. Sorry ta hear it though. What was his work?"

"Had a smithing shop. My sister's husband took it o'er an' I moved on. Our mother was taken by fever two years 'fore.

"I don't mind telling my unexciting story, Mister DeVoe, yet 'twasn't the reason ya asked me ta here, was it?"

"No," I shook my head. "Ya showed yourself a leader t'day, Mister Gorden. What ya spoke would a been better put as a question, yet your words rang right for all ta hear."

"Didn't take Copernicus ta' see it, Mister DeVoe. The line was from the riggin. Plain as day we need line ta trim the sails proper an' run fast. Ya oft say an touch less than our fastest can be fatal. We need line ta tighten ship in rough weather, as well. Especially the way this bobber rides a squall."

"Aye, she's an uncomfortable bobber a' times," I nodded. "A wise new recruit skips a meal when a sizable squall's on the horizon. Yet we all find comfort in her speed. A slow running pirate ship is a fast sinker. This old *Vengeferth* bobs, yet she's built tight, an' we keep a clean hull. She's fore'er held her balance in the worst squall an' come through mast upside."

"She's not so old as that though, is she, Mister DeVoe?"

"Younger 'n most ships a' sea, yet a tad older 'n she looks," I offered. "Stays young due our regular barnacle parties.

"About ya speaking out," I went on. "'Twas the right thing, an' showed a spot a courage, considering Captains state."

"Words jump out. Given time ta think, I mightn't a spoke, though I haven't yet found Captain Werthman one ta fear. Yet his actions against that poor boy give me pause ta wonder."

"Aye, worried me as well. Cookie'd held back the discard two days, so's not ta bring sharks around. An' Evans in the nest 'd kept a shark watch all morn. He gave the Captain a thumb up. Yet it went so awry. The brute came straight up from the depth a hell. 'Twas meant as initiation inta pirate life for the boy. He was ta come up happy an' a touch older. It happened too quick. A sad day, but I can't so much fault the Captain. Yet he's down on 'imself heavy. Feels he's all the blame."

"I hadn't thought on it," Gorden spoke low, facing a' sea. "Considering the intention, he shouldn't let it pull 'im down so far. 'Tis a mean world. Surprise happens. It can jump up in a worst way. We must recognize our sad mistakes, try ta learn, an' move on a touch wiser. 'Twould be a bleak world should we all be seen as no better'n our worst mistake."

"Nicely put, Mister Gorden. I'm far the same mind, an' I expect the Captain'll find his way soon. He's been a level head.

"But the crew leadership's what I asked ya up here ta jaw on. Seems 'tis yours lest ya fight it. Each crew needs a steward, an' ta my mind they could do a damn sight worse 'n yourself."

"I don't really know the ins an' outs, Mister DeVoe. Kolke didn't seem ta do much as steward last trip out. Tell me what's expected an' what the rewards might be?"

(6) Steward's job

"Steward listens ta the crew, jaws with me, an' I pass on some ta the Captain. If there's a problem that wants us three ta jaw together, we do. No need ta think yourself a sneak. Let the men have privacy, but if there's anything begging the Captain's attention or mine, ya pass it on. Any fierce dislikes come up amongst the men, we need ta know. We try ta iron problems smooth 'fore they blow an' crewmen get hurt. Men can get in each other's way on a boat this small. A' times they step on each other's worst wart. Some trips it happens more oft," I chuckled, dumping a bit a pipe's ash down ta the still water, an' recalling the silliness a most disputes. "We've a good crew aboard this time out, yet 'tis the rare trip that nothing comes up.

"A crew leader leads by example. He encourage the men, the way it seems your dad did. Ya wouldn't give orders. Sure, we'd back ya, being 'tis sensible, but still it might turn the crew against ya. A man does something good or extra, ya give 'im a good word. He messes up, ya lightly suggest a lesson ta be learned. Your idea a men being better 'n their worst mistake is fine thinking. Offer words like that ta the crew.

"The men need help, ya give it. Wanna talk, ya listen. They fight, ya get help an' break it up 'fore someone's hurt. Ya get ta know each man. There's plenty ya got ta learn aboard. Let 'em teach ya. Nothing a man likes more 'n showing off what he knows ta someone offering interest.

"Go ashore, y've heard me warn 'em ta' stay in groups after

dusk, so's ta cover each other's backs. Ashore, ya help 'em get inta groups. An' don't wander off on your own lonesome after dusk. You're an example. Ya can't be o'er responsible for 'em though. Have some good time, but keep an eye out a bit. If ya find a chance, break up a fights. I'm around, as well.

"Steward's most *official* job's leading rummage trips. Mind close Captain's words. Each boat's different. Shouldn't go awry if 'tis done right. Cookie's helper, Tom, goes along ta bring back food an' good meat. Doc's man, Sammy, goes ta find science books for Doc's library, an' doctoring stuff, should it be aboard. The rest a the gang are your choices. Try ta pick the right ones. Honest ones who'll fight if need be. Ya wanna pass it around much as ya can though. Give most a the crew a chance ta have the fun, but no hotheads. I've seen none yet this time out.

"Ya went rummaging once last trip out, didn't ya?"

"Aye, Mister Kolke took me rummaging the *Jackfisher*."

"Ah, slim pickins there. Poor refugees. We shouldn't a took it. Captain can most times tell at a distance, but not always," I emptied my ashes, tapped the rail, an' spat. "A richer ship can wear a poor look, hoping ta sneak through. At least ya had the experience, so ya know how it goes. I repeat, each ship's different. Listen close ta me an' the Captain. We've seen 'em all."

"Now, about your swordplay—"

"I'm catching on quite well I feel, Mister DeVoe," Gorden broke in, "an' finding it most enjoyable."

"Yet how many times did ya use it your first trip out?"

"I was learnin, an' mine's been all practice, but nobody aboard got out ta raise a sword."

"Aye. See, I hate ta disappoint ya, but we're unlikely ta use swordplay these days. It takes a far stern seat here. Our magical cannons carry the day. T'day Captain Werthman's fearsome sharpshooting's far known. An' ta be honest, Mister Gorden, our small crew a forty'd stand a pityfull chance with swords against most any ship out there, however skilled we'd be.

"Don't get me wrong. Skill with a blade has a chance a saving your hide one day. Yet too much time spent practicing is near as likely ta cost ya your life from a slip-up. I've seen it twice."

"So my time might be better spent," He pondered.

"Aye, one thing, you're not at home in the riggin the way ya need ta be so's ta help when we scramble up in front of a squall an' time's short. Learning the guns wouldn't hurt as well.

"Ya see, practicing on the swords is fine ta put a body in shape, but being steward or not, ya need ta spread yourself about. On a small ship, men must be jack a all trades. The best are master. 'Tis good the crew enjoys teaching what they know. I take ya as a quick learn. Just spread your time 'round. It'll all come ta ya. Now, 'tis clear you're crew leader if ya want. Do ya see it worth a try?" I feared I'd gone too on an' discouraged 'im.

"Well, clearly ya got it right about me needing ta change my thinking. Been enjoying the swordplay too much. Should a seen it. Yet, being on but my second trip, I'm unsure the crew 'd take ta me as steward. An' being steward seems a bother. More so on a trip begun so poorly," Gorden told. Then, with a smile in his voice, "An' if ya got ta the rewards part, I musta missed it."

"Rummaging trips are more fun than work, Mr. Gorden," I chuckled. "There's few ways ta improve your lot as a pirate. Do well an' ya get the men's respect an' the Captain's too. For some it goes easy, as I'm thinking it would for yourself. Yet the job can test a man's patience an' his metal as well. But 'tis easy 'nough ta step away, if ever ya decide ta do so. An' quite lucky's the man cut out for it, as I'd wager ya are."

"Well, I lean toward it. But I'd like the night ta sleep on it, if ya don't mind."

"Sounds fine. Nothing needs attention tonight. Let's get our rest an' jaw after morn mess. Ya might have more questions."

The sun was down an' all quiet as we went below.

'Twas clear Gorden'd be well cut for leadership, an' was near ready ta step up. Ta the man, I saw the crew being good. An' the Captain seemed ta be coming back ta 'imself. I looked for'rd ta the trip settling down ta normal an' turning easy an' smooth. It seemed so likely, but the vision couldn't a been more off.

(7) 'Twasn't my finest hour

Next morn Captain joined us at early mess, something he did a few times each trip. 'Twas another quieter meal, light chatter clearly not feeling right, an' few finding serious talk ta make. At meal's end Doc stood up an' read a prayer for the boy an' Jonesy. He'd been awake late writing it. 'Twas penned long an' full a every bit a the pain we each held inside. The prayer was pure an' powerfull poetry, an' Doc read it out strong an' well. He was bursting with a deep sorrow, as were all. Poor Willie B broke down midway. Heitman half carried 'im off ta his bunk. The crew's amens came choked out weak.

After some pause, Captain stepped up. "'Twas far from my intention, men, yet I mournfully put the blame on my own foolishness," he started in soft an' low as though speaking ta one close ear. Yet his voice flowed easy ta all, "The boy was meant ta come up alive, happy, an' a little more grown. He'd feel 'imself one a the crew. A

"As for Jonesy, the beast was my fight. I shouldn't a took 'im an' Willie B along. Yet we must put it behind. Intentions may justify my sad mistakes. Any way ya look, 'twasn't my finest hour. Surely my maker'll bring it up when we meet. He'll do me the favor a sorting it all out. Till then, 'tis my duty ta search out better judgement in the future.

"Now, there's deciding ta be done," He went on, stronger. "A reason we all took up this pirate life was ta escape being bossed about so much. Me, same as you. So I'm opening things up ta discussion, as sometimes I do. My plan was for us ta sail east, take one ship, an' then head for a cozy bay an' a barnacle party. Ya know why, same old reasons, keep our best speed, an' our hull strong. But a steady breeze's pouring from the east. 'Tis unusual this time a year in these parts. We'll get less speed sailing east. There are choices. We can sail northwest, west, southwest or work our way east.

"Fact is, I doubt forty men jawing in a room could agree on how ta arrange a shoelace in a month. The ship needs tending.

So I ask that ya vote a steward ta jaw with Mister DeVoe an' me. Send 'im ta my quarters, an' he'll come 'round explaining at mess. I suggest Mister Gorden. He spoke quick an' level headed yesterday when my judgement was sorely clouded. Yet your leader's not my choice. You're good men. I'm fine jawing with any a ya. Me an' Mister DeVoe'll step ta my quarters. Pick a man, send 'im 'round, an' get back ta busy."

Captain's fine talk after mess, like Doc's prayer, felt right as rain. Things were looking up, as the Captain an' me strode for'rd on deck with a clear sky, brisk steady breeze, an' nary a cloud. Bright sun poured o'er the white billowed canvas, pure as heaven's sweet honey.

The ship'd surely been righted an' turned ta smooth sailing, which left me relieved. I looked for an easy trip, as 'twas planned as my last. Captain knew this, but none else aboard did. I was long in the tooth for the pirate game. Felt myself begin ta pull less 'n my weight. Captain claimed not ta agree, but 'twas as I told Gorden, on a small ship hands need ta be good with all skills. I tired a whit quicker an' needed more rests 'n the young chaps. Couldn't climb ta the nest an' stand watch, due ta bleary eyes. Neither could I work the riggin, less 'twas calm. Calm's not when help's needed atop. Facing a squall I was useless as Gorden or a new man. Yet new men catch on. Everybody takes time learning. I was past catching on or catching up.

I wasn't o'er happy about leaving the ship, yet beginning ta feel that standing on dry land wasn't so bad. I spent two years a' shore a time earlier, 'fore Werthman lured me back a' sea. I expected ta pine little for the briny after this crazy tour.

The Captain an' me were in his quarters but two or three minutes setting out his maps when Gorden showed up.

"Well, Mister Gorden, have a seat," Captain greeted 'im warm, nodding ta the third chair in the close room. "'Tis good ta see the men had the sense ta choose a fine steward."

"Thanks, Captain. I'm unsure. Either they wanted me, or none desired the post, an' all were relieved ta put it off on me."

"I think y'll find it ta your liking, Mister Gorden," Captain chuckled, sounding more his old self. "I assure ya there's more good in it than bad. Crew seems right, me an' Wil are more the easy going type, an' ya seem well cut for it. So 'tall feels good."

"I'm not taking the job expecting ta agree every time," Gorden advised, "yet this being but my second trip out, I feel a bit raw ta offer much advice. But we'll see."

"Indeed we'll see. A fresh pair a eyes must be a help. Don't ya fear ta offer an opinion when one feels right. Yesterday I was muddle-headed, an' ya gave a clear truth I needed ta hear. I make mistakes, but I'm hopefull, twixt you an' Wil, they'll be caught 'fore I act on 'em. It doesn't mean I'm not the Captain at the end. We'll disagree a' times. Yet I'll make the effort ta well weigh each opinion 'fore I act. Ya got my word."

(8) Willie B's state a mind

We studied the Captain's maps, jawing on where our *Vengeferth* should take us next on this trip. There was much ta consider, the need ta scrape our hull, the unusual wind, an' more details. I went out ta' see the ship was being well-tended an' get noon mess. Soon after I came back, we settled on a plan Gorden could put 'fore the crew at eve mess.

"The men are likely ta come 'round," Captain assured Gorden. "Don't o'er explain it, but answer all questions. Some may feel the need ta jaw. No secrets in the plan. Mister DeVoe'll be there should ya need help remembering or explaining."

Gorden laid it out well an' clear at mess, so the crew came 'round. 'Twas settled. We'd make our way southwest, down along the Dark Continent's coast, take one more ship, then pull in for a barnacle party. At late mess, Gorden asked me ta the quarter deck. We stepped up there again.

"'Tis been a fine day, Mister Devoe," He started in.

"Most fine," I agreed. "Comforting ta have the ship righted an' aimed at smooth sailing. A course there's no certainty. Each trip turns adventuresome one way or t' other."

"Aye, I suppose," He nodded. "I asked ya up here ta get some small guidance. I plan ta start learning the riggin tomorrow an' wish ta know the crewman best at showing the skills."

"I'm glad ta hear that...hmm. Well, Dessinger 's the best we got working up top, but likely the worst choice as teacher. The riggin comes too easy to 'im. Steps 'round up there like 'tis ballet. The best are oft poor teachers. Not patient enough ta teach even a quick learn like I judge ya ta be. An' there's Johnson. Knows it well, but talks poorly, mostly on account a scarce teeth. None can catch but one in ten words. Cheerfull though.

"I might be best at teaching if I went up. But I don't go up. Eyes bleary. Upshot is Heitman's your man. 'Im an' Barker do the teaching these days, but twixt you an' me, Heitman's the better. Don't mention ya heard it from me. Let Heitman show ya. Be carefull. Rare's the man lives ta tell of a fall, even when he's tied on. Tied on gives a chance but 'tis no guarantee."

"I'll be carefull."

"Expect it ta scare the bejesus out a ya first few times. An' don't get down on yourself for not taking it quick. Nobody does," I spoke seriously. "Y'll get it in your mind long 'fore your muscles get the trust. Finally, a time along, y'll relax some. That's the way it goes. Just never once fully relax atop, least you're tied on in the nest. An' when tied on, be sure you're tied on well. It only means your life."

'Twas quiet between us a bit, like he thought I'd go on forever. I feared I'd already gone too on an' scared 'im off going up. But one must know what ta expect 'fore going up. Gotta be prepared. It starts out scary an' dangerous for every man. Never stops being dangerous.

"Thanks for the good words, Mister DeVoe. I'll keep 'em well in mind when I go up," he assured, an' turned ta step down from the quarter deck only ta find Doc on the steps coming up.

"Good eve gentlemen," Doc greeted us. "Cheers Mister Gorden. Expect you'll do fine as steward. The men chose well."

"Thank ya, Doc," Gorden took Doc's firm handshake an' spoke solemn. "Your prayer was a fine piece. Comforting an' powerfull as could be. I admire ya on it."

"Thank you. It was deeply felt. As the steward, I suggest you stay and hear what I came to tell Mister DeVoe about Willie B."

"Aye, not taking Jonesy's loss easy, is he, Doc?" I offered.

"Not at all. They came aboard together, an' a' times I considered 'em more than friends. Of course it's really no matter. They wouldn't be the first pair closer than friends to sign on aboard a pirate ship to escape society's uncivilized bother."

"Aye. Seemed their bent," I agreed. "If so, they kept quiet. The type's less oft the problem shipboard. 'Tis a too religious bloke in the crew who catches on an' takes affront. Or else a natural bully o'erfull a 'imself an' his loud manliness. Saw it my first trip out. I learned from it, but I don't talk on it."

"Well, anyway," Doc went on, "I doubt Willie'll ever come around to being any help aboard this ship. The best we can do is see that he gets home and find ourselves another man."

"Is it what he's wanting, Doc?" I asked, an drew on my pipe.

"He's too dumbfounded to know what he wants. One minute he's faulting himself for leaving Jonesy on the smallboat, then he turns to blaming himself for having Jonesy sign with him aboard the *Vengeferth*. In his next breath he blames it all on the Captain. He's so sick with trying to place the fault, that he can't hear the truth and feel the comfort in my words."

"Let's put it ta the Captain," I offered, an' we stepped below.

Captain's room was small ta sit four, so back up on the quarter deck Doc told a Willie B's sorrowfull state.

"Doc, ya don't see 'im working past it soon?" Captain asked.

"Best guess is he'll get worse. I'm no doctor of the mind, but he stays in his bunk without asleep. A man who isn't sick, can't sleep, and has little wish to eat, has a troubled mind."

"Can't disagree, Doc. We're going the wrong way ta take 'im home. Let's pay his passage on the next ship we see going east. Getting 'im away from here'd be the best, do ya think?"

"Sounds right."

"What about ya two?" Captain asked, turning ta Gorden an' me for consideration. We nodded in agreement, as it appeared clearly the best way ta go. Yet, in the end, it so sadly failed ta turn out the best way.

(9) A dangerous plan

As we left the quarter deck, Captain asked me ta come by next morn after mess. Arriving I found 'im at his desk. He sat pen in hand, unsmiling o'er a blank paper.

"G' morn Wil. Sad letters should go out ta Jonesy's family an' Willie's too. I'd write 'em, but the last two days left my hand a bit shaky. My script's turned worse than poor. Ya wield the pen an' let's word 'em together. Got ta get 'em done. No telling how quick we'll see a ship ta carry Willie B an' the letters out."

That's how we spent the morn. 'Twas no time enjoyed, but in need a doing by civilized men. We explained things ta families as best we could, leaving out ugly details. Told 'em we couldn't send money with those letter as we didn't trust the messenger. But the men were owed small sums, which we'd expect ta deliver as soon as possible within the year.

I was bothered ta learn the Captain had the shakes. Doc needed ta' know. He might have something for it.

The letters done, Captain sent me ta check the ship an' bring Gorden. We'd stop an' have Doc check Gorden's eyes. All was fine aboard the ship. Had a good crew. Men were keeping busy. Cookie's man, Tom, was bringing noon mess 'round. Heitman assured there was a steady watch for boats on the horizon, 'imself on the quarterdeck an' the man in the nest. Oars ta the powlocks, we were rode lowsails--meaning topsails were down. We rode lowsails searching out ships, so's ta stay hard ta see.

Heitman'd been working with Gorden about an hour. As Gorden stepped away, Heitman gave me a nod, "He'll do in time, Mister DeVoe. He'll likely be near the best one day."

"I'm glad someone feels I'll ever be good in the riggin," Gorden spoke low as he followed me. "I sorely doubt it."

"Didn't I say takes time?" I reminded 'im. "Heitman knows. He's schooled many men, an' knows their measure."

Truth is, 'twas too soon ta know. I helped Heitman encourage an' build confidence. Doc found no fault with Gorden's eyes, an' we went for'rd. Captain seemed in better spirits.

"Doc says his eyes are good as gold," I offered as we entered.

"That's good news. Have seats men. I hear you spent the morn with Heitman, Mister Gorden. How'd it go?"

"Learned a bit, Captain. Can't say I see the good future Mister Heitman sees in me, but I may come 'round in time."

"He got ya up ta the main mast's first yardarm with ya hanging on for dear life I'm sure," Captain chuckled.

"'Twould be a fair description." Gorden smiled, nodding.

"Been there a first time, Mister Gorden. Been there. Did Barker tell ya the first yardarm's not the easiest?"

"No, he didn't mention."

"'Tis true. Men who haven't gone up are sure bottom's the easiest, but most days the second's easier. Neither's an easy biscuit in higher chop. Main thing is ta be tied on no matter the chop, so's ya might live ta tell about a misstep. There's no knowing when the rare crosswave'll hit.

"I'm pleased ta hear you're likely ta catch on ta the riggin, but 'tis not what I asked ya in ta talk on. Fact is, 'tis time I share some a our magical guns' secrets, how they're aimed an' fired so accurately. I see ya as a quick learner. 'Tis neither magic, nor so very hard. Needs but a steady hand an' good eye. Doc knows it all. I'd a taught Mister DeVoe a time back, were his eyes good. Suddenly I lack the steady hand needed for the job. I'm sure 'tis a brief problem, but I've a slight case a the shakes.

"Ya know we plan a friendly meeting with another ship. A course friendly's not our usual sort a meeting. Fact is it could go awry, an' should it, we'll need ta sharpshoot or be done."

"Sounds risky. Do the odds look good?"

"I think so. We'll dust off the Sunday-go-ta-meeting flag we never use, an' keep our distance, but there's scoundrels an' suspicions out there. They could mistake our intentions. Take us for lowlifes trying ta sneak in on 'em. Not all ship Captains know our bent is upright. If we deal with one who knows, it should go well. A friendly meeting means Willie B an' our letters'll get safe passage. I owe Jonesy an' Willie my best try."

"Gotta be honorable ta expect honorable. We'll try ta stay clear a military or pirates, so I think the odds are good it'll go well. If not, we take a ship we hadn't intended. Yet, we'd still have our letters an' Willie B. Can't put 'em on a ship we take.

"Yet we must be prepared should it go bad, else we'll be open ta destruction. Gotta be full ready ta take out their main mast quick. Let's step up ta the quarter deck ta get ya schooled on aiming the guns."

"Do ya really think I'll pick it up so fast? Might we avoid any ship at least a day or two whilst I practice?"

"Nonsense. Fact ya don't know it, doesn't make it hard. Ya need only learn ta set the looking glass. 'Twill take minutes. Can't practice till there's a jib ta focus on. Bigger secrets are in the guns. Y'll learn their workings someday, but ya need know naught a their workings ta aim an' order 'em triggered."

(10) The looking glass

We three stepped ta the quarter deck, Captain ready ta show the working a his looking glass. There Heitman stood with that glass ta his eye, scouring the horizon.

"Mister Heitman, I'm about ta share the secrets on how ta use that glass ta aim the guns. I'm thinking it might be good for ya ta join in an' pick up the skill as well. Never know when we might need another man 'round able ta do the job."

"More 'n happy ta learn, Captain. I've been curious on it. For a time it's been my small worry that ya might someday be indisposed whilst the guns need aiming."

"Doc's known of it for a time. 'Tis best more knew."

He took a round piece a glass from his pocket an' fixed it just so, inta the middle a the looking glass. Then he set it out. How ta focus on a distant object, then read numbers on the glass's barrel an' learn the distance a what's in focus. He went on ta show how one must line up the glass ta aim the guns side ta side. As expected, my eyes weren't able ta find the focus in the looking glass, an' the small numbers on the barrel blurred, though I did get the feel a how it worked together so well. The others had sharp eyes for it, an' much surprise at its ease.

"Ya thought my sharpshooting with the cannons showed me

a wizard or genius," he smiled. "Didn't ya, men?

"'Tis the enjoyed power a knowledge. If ya don't let the crew on ta its ease, we'll all be wizards," he chuckled. "This fine instrument came from the East an' shows their genius, not mine. Any genius I might have's in the guns. Me an' my brother gleaned the secrets in our cannons an' their strangely shaped balls. One day I expect ta have the pleasure a sharing the secrets a the guns with ya o'er a nice big feast.

"Y'll get practice when there's a jib ta focus on. Be quick ta drop the sails when one's spotted," Captain finished, took his round glass from the looking glass, an' put it in his pocket. He strode ta his quarters, whilst Gorden stayed on the quarter deck scouring the distance. Me an' Heitman went about the ship's business together, mostly checking all was ready for the meet up. We had ta be well prepared should it go unfriendly.

'Twas my relief that he shared the secrets a the looking glass. Heitman wasn't the only crewman who'd held the worry a something happening ta the Captain, thus leaving us with fine cannons we couldn't aim so well. I should a known he'd share the secrets with Doc. In his room, Doc even had a little round glass piece, same as that in Captain's pocket.

(11) A speck on the horizon

An hour after we left Gorden, I was heading ta my room for ta read when he called out from the quarter deck, "Jib ho, thirty two degrees port! Drop sails!"

Evans, up in the nest, was silent a time 'fore calling down, "Can't find her sir! Be ya dead sure?"

"Stay on it," Gorden called. "A tick past thirty degrees."

Captain's priceless looking glass was tied on at the quarter deck. 'Twas too risky ta allow it in the nest. The looking glass up top was a tad poorer. Yet the height a the man in the nest oft made up for the disadvantage. 'Twas always a competition ta see which'd first find a speck on the horizon. Mister Gorden had a bragging good eye if he'd picked up a speck Evans couldn't find after he was given the location. Unless 'twas dust on Gorden's glass, or he dreamed it. He sounded certain.

Me an' the Captain reached the quarter deck, Heitman a step behind. 'Twas no running matter. No hurry needed, as sails were down. Evans in the nest hadn't called it yet, so there was doubt Gorden'd seen more 'n a dirt speck on his glass.

"Ya still on it?" the Captain asked as we arrived.

"Still on it, Captain."

"What kind a ship da ya make it?"

"Still a speck. Be a time 'fore we fathom that, sir."

"Let Mister Heitman give it a look."

Gorden handed the looking glass o'er, an' Heitman agreed, "Aye, a speck all right. Likely a ship, but 'tis yet uncertain."

Evans called, "Found her!" as the Captain had oarsmen turning us thirty two degrees ta face the speck. *Vengeferth* had four powlocks with long oars in on each side. Two to the oar could move her along smartly. With our canvas down, it'd be a time 'fore they saw us coming on. We wished ta learn the type a ship we dealt with 'fore we were seen. *Vengeferth* was hard ta spot coming straight on without canvas. Ships we took, a' times saw us so late as ta swear we'd jumped from the sea like magic.

We'd no wish ta take this ship, just flee quick, were it military or a pirate ship. The sooner we cut an' ran, the better. Particularly from military, who had more an' bigger guns. At a distance, their aim was laughable poor, but should he throw plenty a balls, even a blind man's bound ta get lucky.

"Mister Heitman, give the glass o'er ta Mister Gorden an' head down," Captain ordered, as Doc arrived on the quarter deck. "Get the peace flag up, an' have the oarsmen ease ta three quarters. Tire yourself a bit on an oar, then step back up ta man the glass, so's Gorden can go down an' take a turn on an oar. Don't know what we have here yet. Tell the oarsmen ta save some muscle ta run out, should we have the need."

"I'll relieve an oar, Captain," Doc offered. "Muscles need a stretch. It'll feel good to pull my weight for a change."

"Ya pull your weight 'round here fine, Doc. Yet it'd be a good idea an' appreciated. First take a turn at the glass an' work with

Evans an' Gorden at figuring out what kinda ship 'tis. My shaking hands are no good on the glass t'day."

They soon came ta the agreement that the speck was truly a ship. I remarked ta Doc that Gorden's eye was good as gold, likely better. Doc nodded an' headed down ta take an oar. It grew ta a speck for the naked eye ta see--all but mine that is-- whilst the men at the looking glasses called their views back an' forth. Gorden was the first ta say *military*. Captain didn't need ta hear the word twice.

"Lift oars!" He boomed. That quick we were adrift. "Guns?"

"Aye. Twelve on deck, this side. Likely a row beneath."

"Give it a look, Heitman," Captain told. Then ta the nest, "Seeing guns, Evans?"

"Just picking 'em up, Captain. Too many. Let's git."

"Heitman, ya got 'em as well?"

"Aye, they're there, Captain," he agreed. "But she has the cut of a freighter, so 'tis less than certain they're real."

"Think they might be wood?"

"Might be a freighter showing wooden ones ta trick folks like us an' scare us off, Captain. She likely has real ones on the corners an' a few mixed in. Either 'tis a freighter turned military with lots a real guns, or a freighter trying ta look military carrying some wood guns ta scare us off."

(12) The *Daisy Belle*

"They might be wood guns?" Gorden asked by my ear.

"Aye, they're shown ta scare us off, yet cheap an' light, so's the ship can carry full cargo."

"How close must ya be ta tell wood from real?" he asked me.

"Ya must stand there beside 'em. They're painted with the same paint, so's the two look alike from any distance."

"No flag up on her yet?" Captain asked loud, an' the men on both glasses answered none.

"Captain, is there no way ta tell wood guns?" Gorden asked.

"None, lest ya see one carried on a bloke's shoulder."

"Can we stay outside gun range an' send in a smallboat?"

"That'd be a long smallboat trip in this cross chop. More'n a bit uncertain. As steward, y'd be in the boat, Mister Gorden. What's ta be done should ya founder? Send out another smallboat ta get in trouble with ya? Or go out ta save ya, thus endanger the ship in range a their guns?

"Ya seem ta have the best eye aboard t'day, Mister Gorden," he went on. "They've set no flag, so haven't spotted us. Or they *pretend* not ta see us. Study her whilst we row on at quarter speed. In about thirty minutes we reach the edge a gunning range. 'Twill be decision time. By then they're sure ta spot us, but ya might figure it out. Wood guns or real. I dislike being scared off by wood guns, but 'twould be no fun seeing a dozen cannon balls coming our way. I'll take less chance whilst trying ta be' peaceable an' do the right thing."

Captain called for quarter speed from the oarsmen, whilst Gorden's eye pressed ta the looking glass.

Been around a time, so I knew Captain's considerations. We were small with great guns an' sails down. Facing for'rd at her, we had fine advantage should a fray start. We were the much smaller target ta hit, with fine aim in our guns. Yet we had aloft a peace flag an' wanted no fray. The day's stiff crosswind cost our guns some small accuracy, whilst, if we got in range an' she threw a full volley at us, she might get lucky.

If we circled an' faced her stern, we'd get around the crosswind, thus improve our aim, an' give our smallboat an easy trip across. Yet on her backside, we'd face her biggest guns, an' we couldn't so quickly cut an' run with a tail wind blowing us at her. Also, whilst running out from behind her, we must, for a short time, show our broadside inside her gun range.

Gorden said they were dropping sails. We were seen. She'd leave up no sails. No chance she could outrun us. In a fray, she want no cannonballs chewing up her canvas.

"Flag yet?" Captain asked.

"Seems they're readying one, sir...Aye, 'tis a peace flag."

"An' she's turning?"

"Aye, Captain," Gorden observed.

"What about the guns?"

"It appears some may have cracks saying they're wood, as Heitman guessed, but not the end ones," came Gorden's reply. "I'm not certain enough ta bet my life on it though."

"Fine. We stay outside cannon range swinging upwind. Gotta hurry, daylight's wasting."

She gave us every advantage an' showed each sign a friendliness. All sorts a tricks yet could be tried. We stayed out a cannon range an' moved upwind. Evans, down from the nest, took the looking glass, whilst Gorden went ta ready his boat crew. Doc assisted Willie B along. A stiff dose a laudanum meant he had ta be half carried ta the smallboat an' tied on so's he wouldn't bounce out. There was no other way he'd go there. Not with what happened last time he sat in that boat.

The wind an' chop were easing down as the six pushed off. Four ta oars moved 'em smartly. We sat upwind facing her broadside, with every advantage. Rested just inside gun range. The chop was easing down as they reached the ship. 'Twas the *Daisy Belle*. I'll ne'er forget *that* name.

(13) Engaging the *Daisy Belle*

Gorden carried three flags, two white an' one red, each with a black corner. He was ta hoist 'em, once aboard. The flags'd tell Captain Werthman about the greeting Gorden met. Black corners a the flags could be turned in any direction. Gorden an' the Captain knew their code. Worst was if no flags went up. Surest sign of trouble. Captain had guns lined up on the *Daisy Bell's* mainmast an' on her mizzenmast, just in case.

Waiting for the flags ta go up was worry time. We weren't taking this ship, just acting peaceable, so ya think it'd go smooth. Yet many suspicions an' tricks were out there. They could suspect trickery in us, as we feared theirs. We knew naught about this *Daisy Belle*, not even her Captain's name.

'Twas growing late. Sun'd soon slide down behind the *Daisy Belle*. We'd sent a smallboat out late. No chance on a return trip 'fore dark. When we took ships, 'twas in late morn, leaving time ta get business all squared away by eve.

"Flags out!" Doc finally called.

"How do they look?" Captain Werthman quick asked.

"Top flag's white with its black spot at the bottom beside the pole. Second's the red one with its spot atop away from the pole. Bottom white has its spot at the top away from the pole."

"An' the flag's spacing. How's that, Doc?"

"Top two close together. Bottom a bit below."

"How far below?" The Captain questioned.

"About enough room for one flag twixt the lower two.

Captain announced things went well with the boarding party, an' all cheered. They'd be back in the morn. He asked me ta set up steady watch an' went ta eat. Steady watch means two men watching. One or two pair a eyes on the *Daisy Belle* at all times. I set it up with the men. 'Twas a clear night with a near full moon. There'd be no trouble keeping steady eyes on her.

Captain asked me an' Doc ta his cabin after mess. We found 'im less cheerfull than he'd been whilst eating with the men.

"So Captain," Doc started, "what more'd Gorden's flags say?"

"We were right about the row a guns on deck being mostly wood, yet she has strong gunnage. Her Captain's been civil, but the gap twixt the middle an' bottom flags means Gorden's not trusting 'im yet. 'Tis good. Don't want 'im o'er trusting. I worry how real his worries might be. Says sharpshooting in the morn would be good. We'll waste a cannonball. You men'll line up the shot, not me. Won't be a problem, right doc?"

"No. We'll handle it. But I'm a bit worried about your shaking, Captain. I'd like ta do a few tests. See if we can figure out the problem. I may be able to do something about it."

"In a day we'll be away from the *Daisy Belle,* an' I invite the testing, Doc. I'd much like ta know the problem myself.

"Mister DeVoe, have the watch keep oars in the powlocks. They should keep us facing her. An' tell 'em don't let her closer without me knowing. We're too quick for 'em ta run away. Worst'd be waking ta find her sidled up ta us, guns staring down our throat. I'll be at the helm shortly 'fore dawn."

(14) Target practice

We mentioned g'nights an' went for sleep. Captain was in a state. Surely his eyes didn't close all night. I checked the watch, then went ta my room. In search a sleep, I found little.

The usual order a business when we took ships was for 'em ta surrender 'fore we began shooting down their masts. Our deadly accurate cannons were far known. After their surrender, their Captain must row o'er an' come aboard as guest hostage. Then we sent out a rummaging gang. 'Twas well known business, an' went easy as a biscuit most oft.

Through the night I kept seeing all that could go awry, putting our men aboard the other boat whilst we held no hostage in kind. Anything might happen ta the men after Gorden put up those flags saying all was well. Treacheries could be imagined. From bellies full a poison ta knives in bellies. Gorden's morn signal flags'd tell if all stayed well through the night. Treachery by her Captain in the night meant we'd take off *The Daisy Belle's* masts one by one, then put two at her water line ta send her down. But sadly it wouldn't bring back our men. 'Twas the longest a nights.

I stepped ta the deck at dawn an found Captain Werthman looking like death warmed o'er. He beat me there by a few minutes. 'Twas a beauty of a cloudless sunrise who's perfection we couldn't enjoy. Then Gorden's flags flew. Evans described the flags, an' Captain assured all seemed well.

"Fact is," Captain laughed, smoothing his brim, "we'll eat well. They wagered some fine food that we'll miss the target."

All cheered an' laughed. More cheers came when Evans called from the nest, "Putting out a target, Captain. Two men paddling a boat an' pulling something. Seems kinda small. Let's see...looks like three a their wooden cannon barrels are lashed together with a red flag sticking a few foot up."

"Small. Can ya hit her?" Captain asked Heitman at the glass.

"No doubt in this low chop," came his answer.

"Aye. Line gun two up tight on the target. When the small boat's clear, an' your aim's set, give the signal. Lots a time. No hurry. Check that our other guns are well aimed on their masts 'fore ya fire on the target. No hurry. Take lots a time."

Captain called for quiet, whilst Doc an' Heitman took time passing the glass back an' forth calling ta the gunners. Then Doc yelled go, an' she roared her throaty growl. The ship bucked, an' a smoke ring went up slow like one an old pipe smoker might send toward the ceiling. Crew held their noise an' their breath. Till even my bleary old eyes saw the red flag pop up spinning atop a spout a water. We'd landed one so close in front. Not as dead on as Captain planned, yet perhaps better, as we sent the red flag spinning high for all ta see. 'Twas a fine show well cheered.

"A touch short," Captain growled low.

"Aye," Doc an' Heitman nodded.

"But she sure was pretty!" Captain then crowed, in loud praise. His eyes singing, he wore a wide smile an' slapped backs.

Gorden told me later that the ship's Captain suspected the stories a our deadly shooting a being just that, stories. Or at the least, exaggerations. Gorden told 'im our guns had the aim ta take down masts each by each, then put holes at the water line. Surely that Captain's doubts went down with our cannon ball when it sent his red flag flying up like a whale's blowhole.

Soon Gorden an' the men came rowing back. Moving slow. When they were half way, Evans called that they appeared weighted down with a quarter a beef an' two sizable sacks, likely potatoes. That got the crew's next cheer a the morn.

(15) All goes awry

The world felt rolling so right. Great beauty a the morn was lightbreezing through. *Thank ya Lord,* whispered in throats, with glances ta heaven. Last night's fretting'd been found a waste. 'Twas sleep poorly lost, an' we the tired for it.

With loud cheers we winched the smallboat up, heavy with meat an' potatoes. Yet 'twas the moment, as it swung o'er the rail, Evans' painfull shrill call screeched down from the nest.

Wallllll!!!

~ 38 ~

A second's prayer in my head begged I'd misheard 'im scream squall. But all the raw fear'd ripped through his voice. Hair on necks prickled, as eightysome eyes flew ta the horizon. *Port bow,* was gasped an' heads swiveled. My bleary eyes espied a silver sword blade stretching across the horizon, sparkling in the sun. These knuckles whitened clasping the rail, as my knees tried ta buckle.

"Four ta the oars! The rest below!" Captain barked. **"Tighten ship, douse candles, an' hug a bed leg! Batten down all but aft hatch! Doc, raise the weather flag 'fore ya go down!"** his words rang, quick, sharp, an' loud, like sword clangs in a hot fray.

The briny boasts some thousand ways ta reach out an' tear the life from your gut. Sharks live always hungry. Y've seen one charge up from the bowels a hell ta snatch a tasty snack. Then there's squids, snakes, eels, gators, an' such that rarely take a liking ta ya--only once, given a chance. Other beasts roam so deep they go unnamed, but for swearword names on final breaths. Ice chunks in the fog can cozy up an' rend your hull, bow ta stern, appearing sparkly white an' innocent. An' spritely water spouts dance a' times on waves, as coy as comely lasses, yet if one goes full grown, she'll twirl ya on a short path up ta heaven, or screw ya down ta hades if 'tis where you're expected. Chance a surviving such scourges is most slim, yet does exist.

Then there's a wall. The ocean's most seldom, yet certain, grim reaper. Sailors whisper 'tis the hand a God sweeping all the crumbs from the table ta the floor.

'Tis a mammoth wall a water, wide an' tall, that charges madly 'cross the sea, like a raging bull. I *do* mean wide an' tall. The span may be vast beyond estimation. Height might go two ships. Measurements are guesswork, fathomed from results. A wall rushes fearsome fast at brains too far befuddled ta consider its measure. Minutes spent facing a wall are meant for making peace with God, not finding measure sticks. Yet should a soul find time an' means ta measure, who'd hear?

Crumbs on the ocean floor don't talk.

A strongest Captain facing a wall might melt inta bread pudding, an' a mealy mouth turn ta a giant. No knowing the best action. 'Tis guesswork that ya go at her like the worst squall.

Walls go unmentioned a' sea for fear the utterance might bring one on. 'Tis a fury spoke on a' sea only when a man climbs ta his first watch. The nest man must know the worst case an' how it may appear.

Yet its appearance, as well, is uncertain. The accepted notion is that coming *from* the sun a wall shows as a black shadow. Whilst rolling *towards* the sun, she shimmers white, reflecting sun in your eyes. Running crosswise ta the sun, mayhap black on one end an' white at the other. 'Tis as good a guess as any. 'Neath a clouded sky she'll likely go unnoticed, ta be first seen looking down on ya. 'Tis better she should find ya smiling in night dreams a your comely lass back home.

Captain Werthman faced it strong. Four oarsmen turned the *Vengeferth* ta face her head on, an' he tied the helm ta stay the course. Alerted by our weather flag, *Daisy Belle* was shedding canvas. All crew, but for Captain, myself an' the oarsmen, were below tightening ship--pulling in guns, lockin, 'em down, an' closing portals. They secured all but the aft hatch, as ordered.

"**Ta the deck guns!**" Captain bawled. Thus far he'd shown quick, bright thinking, but going for'rd ta the deck guns was a puzzlement. No time ta question, or explain. Near six minutes, best guess. We five followed 'im, running full out. Staring us in the face, the white wall'd grown fearsome huge.

"**Unlock an' turn 'em 'round!**" Captain roared.

Had he lost his wits? Cannons with wheels aloose in a squall were a worst danger. They rolled about on pitching decks, busting ships ta kindling. But none argued. No time for questions. None for answers. I held ta my faith that his mind wasn't addled. He didn't shake, an' spoke with certainty a voice. We unlocked an' turned both guns double quick.

"**Stand clear!**" Captain spat, aimed gun two, an' hit her trigger. Thankfully, the guns had no time-eating fuses. She boomed quick an' deafening. That cannonball took out the lower main yardarm's left side, whilst the gun's kick thrust it back through the rail an' down. Its splash washed my neck cold.

As the ball flew, Captain jumped ta quick aiming gun one. The second ball hit the main mast. She tilted, an' o'er she went. Took with her the starb'rd rail. Pitching back, gun one joined her mate in the deep.

"**Ta the hatch!**" he spat. We'd already bounded that way.

Me, the slowest afoot, awaited a turn at the hatch. A glance o'er my shoulder caught the *Daisy Belle* cowering 'fore the wall. It soared above her like a cobra, hood widespread. She sat free a canvas, yet sadly broadside ta the wall an' beginning ta slide sideways down inta the trough 'fore the looming monster's tons a pityless fury. This brain forgot its fear an' went frozen, precariously enthralled. My wide eyes were prisoner a the awesome spectacle playing out so grandly 'fore me. Till, sudden jerked by the Captain, I dove below.

He jumped in behind an' shut the hatch. "Two with DeVoe. Two with me," he barked. "Douse candles, an' hug bed legs."

Several strides ta my quarters, candle snuffed, an' we were three neath my bed. Each wrapped around a leg. 'Twas time for prayer. We felt the *Vengeferth* tilt an' begin her sad descent inta the trough 'fore the wall.

Somehow a mob a thoughts found time ta crowd my craze-filled head. Strangely the words *good* an' *luck* ran through my mind on the brink a this least fortunate moment.

Good luck Evans in the nest set eyes on the monster when 'twas but a broad line on the horizon, giving us needed minutes ta ready. Good luck Evans' mind fathomed what his two eyes beheld, an' neither his terrified mind nor trembling throat froze 'fore screeching the blood-curdling word. Good luck we had no stitch a canvas ta bring down. Good luck the Captain found sense an' time ta turn our bow ta the monster wall. Good luck we kept a strong hull. Far unlike some merchant ships we took, floating coffins, teetering on the gravehole's edge. But ta say *teetering,* here we were tipping 'fore the monster wall, as ta kneel begging mercy from a raging tyrant. My gut shriveled.

Good luck was ta fight bad luck for our very life's breath.

I'd felt our cringing vessel slide down for'rd a long while, then she quick turned her bow up an' all went crazywild. Things untieddown were heard an' felt flinging about. Our *Vengeferth* was slow spinning sideways, pointed bow up an' rising upward for the longest time. Then she sudden flipped ta a jolting loud *kathwump,* with much screeching most painfull ta the ear. That quick we were topsy-turvy, clinging at the floor-turned-ceiling. Our tired *Vengeferth* shuddered like an old dog. She creaked an' settled. All went finally still, an' too silent.

I let out my air an' began ta breathe again.

(16) Flipped

Inta the black I asked low, "Ya men staying alive?"

Both answered A*ye*, an' one moved. At that, my bed broke aloose, an' we crashed, splashing ta the ceiling in ink blackness. 'Twas barely more 'n a six foot fall, but didn't feel good.

I was aches an' pains', bruises an' scratches, but nothing felt broke, an' I didn't feel ta be losing much blood. I was but half sure. 'Twas a dark cow's stomach. My sweat poured, though the air felt cool. Air thick with pickle brine smell. Most darknesses have small light a man's eyes slowly find, but not this.

I again asked, "Ya men staying alive?" an' got but one *Aye*.

We fumbled around, hoping our third man'd only been put cold by the fall, till we found 'im lifeless. Neck broke. Sad. He'd gone through a most chilling confusion the world might throw at a soul, ta then lose life in a drop six foot ta the ceiling.

A distant voice called in the hallway, an' my young partner quick strode toward the door answering. At the doorway I heard 'im kick the frame's top, stretching now at the bottom. His voice cut mid word, an' he pitched through the inky dark ta loudly crash inta the wall across. Quiet again.

I knelt an' groped, splashing toward 'im on all fours. *Another broke neck,* groaned in my mind. He spat just as I found 'im. If not his neck, something must be broke. I checked 'im. His yelp came as I touched the right wrist. Knocked silly an' groaning, he struggled ta his feet with my help. He spat again, an' a tooth splashed in the ankle deep water.

"We'll find Doc ta fix your arm," I offered.

He moaned an' spat another tooth, *plop*.

Voices called in the passage for'rd, then the Captain's voice from aft, low yet so near as ta startle, "Wil, ya alive an' well?"

"Fairly well, Captain," I moaned. "Seen better days, yet nothings broke nor bleeding bad I think. An' yourself?"

"Just stunned. Fuzzy headed. She knocked me cold. My face in the water woke me. I wasn't out long I think. Ankle hurts, but pretty sure 'tis not broke. How about the men with ya?"

"One broken neck. Other's right here. He gave the crash ya just heard. Stumbled headlong inta the wall. Broke his arm an' lost teeth. How about your two oarsmen?"

"Didn't make it. Found 'em lifeless. O'erloaded by us three, my bed broke aloose as we flipped. Don't know how I made it."

Voices called from far for'rd, an' then came Doc's voice nearer, "Do I hear the voices of Captain an' Devoe? I'm certain this isn't heaven. Is this hell, or are we alive?"

"Aye, dark enough for hell," Captain grunted, "but clearly we still live, Doc. How'd ya come out a the tumble?"

"Battered, lost a tooth, shoulder's out. Good, considering."

"Aye, considering," Captain agreed with a chuckle. "Let's look up on your man so's he can turn your shoulder back in."

"Just what I had in mind, Captain."

Doc an' Cookie's helpers shared the room beside Doc's. We four splashed for'rd groping our slow, blind way, feeling along the walls a the pickle-juice-smelling passage, tripping o'er each other some. Doc an' the oarsman hung back so's not ta get their injuries jostled. The broken armed man yipped aloud twice bumping it his own self. I'd ask his name, but his mouth was too bashed for talking. I knew the men well enough. I'd know 'im when I saw his face, if 'twasn't too battered an' swollen.

We reached the door seeking Doc's helper. No answer came ta our pounding. The door'd stayed shut through the wild confusion, but' its frame must a moved crooked ta jam it. Wasn't enough strength in us ta jar it open. We were too beat up an' weary ta give it our best go. As we quit trying, men we'd heard call from down the way came sloshing up ta help. All able bodies gave her another try an' the door gave way. Nobody considered the top frame was now at the bottom. We went tripping tumbling in, painfully adding ta our many bruises an' scrapes. Yelps an' groans echoed about as we flew in, then swear words as we slowly unpiled our tangled selves.

We searched the room, especially up above both beds still attached ta the floor, (now become the ceiling). Nobody was found. Room'd been empty till we came crashing in. Later we found both Cookie's an' Doc's helpers down with Cookie in his room by the galley, the three sadly lifeless, like most aboard.

"Does anybody know about turning a shoulder back to its socket?" Doc asked, as we slowly an' most sorely stumbled from the room. He, with his shoulder aloose, an' the man with a broke arm had waited outside in the hall, unable ta help.

"Had it done ta myself a few years back," was offered.

Gorden's voice. I heaved a sigh. Doc, Gorden, an' Captain Werthman were alive. Surely we'd survive this mess an' reach dry land. They were the cut a men ya knew could pull us out.

"And what's your name?" Doc asked

"Gorden, sir."

"Ah, 'tis you. I should have recognized the voice. How'd you fare, Gorden? Are you sound of body?"

"Bruised an' sore, yet nothing serious, Doc. But shouldn't ya be the one ta turn the man's shoulder back in?"

"Certainly should, but my shoulder's the one out. It's possible to do the procedure for one's self, but I'd prefer not. It's a simple pull and twist. If you've experienced it, you know. The only question is, have you the stomach for it?"

"No problem there, sir. Just worried I can do her right."

"You'll do fine. Don't worry."

We soon found candles an' lit one with Doc's snap lighter. By the low light, Gorden turned Doc's shoulder back in. I might give a clear picture, but must admit ta turning my face ta keep my stomach down. The popping noise an' Doc's loud groan nearly got me anyways.

"Oh, it feels so much better," Doc rasped through tight clamped teeth. Were I a different sort, I might kiss you for it."

"Aye," Gorden allowed. "An' I might slap ya silly. A handshake when yer able'll do." They chuckled in the face a chaos.

In the candle's flicker Doc's sweaty pale face was grim. Four lit candles soon showed all our' faces so dark gray ugly.

"Spread about, men. Search out any who might be alive," Captain urged. "Stay two together ta help each other. Share a candle ta save 'em. If ya see more candles pocket 'em. Any soul found with life, bring ta Doc's room. He'll be working on this man's broke arm. Don't dally. We waded in half a foot, now 'tis nearer a foot. Likely some deck hatches sprung leaks when she flopped. Must be mostly holding though, else water'd be coming up faster. Be most carefull not ta start a fire with a candle. A fire makes us dead men. Gorden, come with me ta check the gun ports. That may be how we'll get out if we make it."

The Captain's *if* iced my spine, but truly a next day felt weakly promised.

(17) Captain Werthman's plan

I partnered with young Dessinger, sloshing through a dank, dismal scene. Hull-side-up, with confusion an' death floating through, 'twas a vision tearfull ta eyes that'd known her with affection. She felt foreign. Already sunk. Dark enough ta be in the depths, peopled with friend's bodies who'd float cold through my sweats long nights later. I was far beyond tired an' began feeling beyond repair. Hell couldn't be worse.

With our candle flickering, we searched the ugly chaos, most uncertain why each body we found was lifeless. I suspected fear-caused heart failure on most accounts.

We gave it up. Seemed hours later, but 'twas much less, we sloshed back ta Doc's room with naught but empty hands.

Other searchers found one surviving soul. Deeply unconscious. Doc held small hope for 'im. Should a known his name, but beaten faces were taking on a ghastly look in the flickering candles. I mightn't a known myself in a mirror.

Captain an' Gorden returned. We gathered in the passage outside Doc's door.

"We checked gun ports an' hatches. None'll open out easy. I feel we'd do best escaping out a gun port," Captain advised.

"Wouldn't opening a hatch be easier, sir?" was asked.

"Aye, easier I expect," Captain nodded. "For'rd hatch's been jarred aloose an' leaks. But open it, an' we'll get water flow hard ta swim through. Most important, going down through there, we could rescue little from the ship. We likely won't last long up top if all our needs go lost."

"Aren't gun portal's small for moving things out? And won't cannons block the way?" came Doc's voice.

"Good thoughts, Doc. I think a cannon's blast blowing a portal out should leave a hefty breach. If need be, we'll unloose the gun from her cleats, an' she'll clear away.

Heads nodded. His plan seemed promising. None faulted it. 'Cept Doc, considered, "Can the guns fire upside down?"

"Well Doc, we made 'em with such a thing farthest from our minds, but I'm dead certain they will," Captain avowed.

"Will the cleats locking it to the ceiling hold?" Gorden asked.

"I'm unsure. The kickback might send her back an' down, but that'd just clear the way. Were she ta plunge through the deck, the *Vengeferth* might follow quick, yet we should have time ta swim free an' bring out some needs."

Again heads nodded.

"Surely there's other ways ta escape this prison, even more sure ones, but we need quick," Captain explained. "Flotsam, maybe even smallboats, float atop. But all's steady scattering. Take some time, a wind comes up, an' we arrive able ta find little ta use. It'd be a tough go. The quicker we move, the better our chance a finding debris, with daylight enough ta gather it.

"Let's prepare. Two ta the galley find tools ta open kegs. Open all holding their seal. Empty 'em by near half, an' use candle wax ta reseal 'em. Thus they'll float high. Lash two kegs together, ten foot a line twixt, an' they'll carry out food, an' line for fashioning a raft. Plenty a kegs in the hold. I hope most didn't bust when we flipped. As they're ready, stow 'em in for'rd rooms near the starb'rd portal. She's the gun we'll blow. Collect candles, line, an' any needs we can push out in the kegs."

"Captain," Gorden offered, "let's wrap foul weather gear an' such 'round kegs. They'll still float whilst carrying clothing."

"Aye, fine thinking. In the galley be sure ta fetch Cookie's meat hammer. In the hold, watch for the keg a nails. If ya step on 'em, be glad they're found, an' pocket many. Let's move."

Some slogged room ta room through the murky, ugly scene searching out needs. Others opened an' resealed kegs, lashing 'em together, then carting 'em ta rooms near the gun port. Captain was dead right. Were they pushed out full, most'd likely go down or hang below the surface. We'd lose any that didn't ride high. Luck was with us. Many were unbroke. They'd been secured against the jostle a storms, but with no thought a the ship going upside down. Fortunately they were tough kegs. Many small ones were whole. Few larger ones held.

(18) Escape

Three quick hours we bustled about, readying. Time speeds when ya have little. A worry niggled at the back a my brain. Our cannon blast's noisy'd go far a' sea, as sounds do. Such loudness is known ta bring sharks nosing about, searching a free meal. Might they greet us in droves? Mayhap the monster wall'd knocked 'em off their usual. We'd soon see.

We waded through thigh-deep water when Captain gathered us all around. "Time ta blow her, men," he declared. "First, four'll go atop, scout the scene, an' gather wood, line, oars, canvas, an' such. Most hopefully, smallboats. If none, lash masts, kegs, an' planks together as a raft. Four below'll push out the kegs. I'll stay here. DeVoe, organize above.

"Doc, how's the man in your room?"

"He didn't make it, Captain."

"'Tis too bad. Yet I saw little chance we'd get 'im out.

"Find hiding spots now, men. Be a wall or two away from her an' not straight behind. She might break aloose, go back, an' take a wall out. Hold your ears. She'll be loud," he shouted o'erloud, as he'd donned the gunners' thick muffs. He was pulling out the safety firing lock. Lord help 'im should she break aloose. Quick as she triggers, ya couldn't get a half step away. Standing off ta her side mightn't help.

We seven scattered. The gun'd been loaded ta fire on the *Daisy Belle* if need be. *Vengeferth* trembled surprising little when she blew. The blast was **terr**ible loud! Echo chased after echo around the doomed ship a longest time an' through my already aching head. Should a woke the dead.

"Four out quick!" Captain coughed in the smoke. His luck held. The gun didn't rip aloose. I pulled myself out through the ingushing water. Dessinger, Gorden, an' the broke armed man came behind me. 'Twas a fine large breach. Six foot ta the surface an' sudden blinding midday sun. I'd forgot how thick the darkness was inside. Fresh air tasted sweet, filling aching lungs, no smoke or pickle brine smell.

My squinting eyes viewed a peacefull scene. No chop, an' much flotsam scattered afar. It appeared as a field after the battle. 'Twas a battle fought, yet whether there'd be a winner was in question. I scanned for shark fins an' found none...yet.

"I'm seeing a boat," Gorden called.

I followed his gaze, an' thirty foot out a smallboat floated upright, yet awash to where only the rail could be seen.

"Quick ta her," I urged an' swam. Behind us we heard kegs popping up. The men below were keeping busy.

We swam near the low craft an' peered in. She had four benches, three of 'em sat four men across, an' the narrower one up front sat two. Benches were sound, but the hull not quite. She had a hefty breach middle bottom.

"No good. No way ta fix her hull," I despaired. "Some shark protection though, should she stay afloat."

Upon seeing that hull's breach, Gorden's eyes lit up. "If she can stay afloat a short time," he avowed, "she'll be riding high well 'fore the sun sets."

"How's that?" I asked. "Have ya the means ta fix her?"

"We'll wrap her like the king's birthday gift!" He cried.

Gorden later told me his confidence was less than he let on. The idea seemed our best chance, yet a hope as low as the craft.

"'Tis the way. Give orders," I urged, having no plan myself.

"Nobody touch her. She might go down. Dessinger, go back an' send out Reed, our slightest man, with four kegs for bailing. They needn't be perfect. Good'll do. We'll fetch the sail hanging ta the yardarm o'er there. Pray it lacks holes."

Gorden an' me went for the sail. The broke arm man stayed. Reed soon brought out the kegs an' pitched 'em inta the foundering craft. Gorden then sent 'im under ta ease 'imself through its breach. A tight squeeze, but none dared roll o'er the side for fear a tipping her. Reed stayed afloat inside. Half a touch might send her down. As we worked the canvas close under her, Gorden's plan finally fell together in my head. We pulled the tarp edges up till they were o'er the rail an' inside. Reed turned ta fiercely bailing, an' she soon raised a bit.

Splashes an' Captain's sputtering voice reached my ear as Gorden pointed out a fin cutting waves. The shark wasn't so close, but no distance in the wide ocean is far enough from a shark whilst your skinny legs hang down as food.

"Good enough," Gorden called. "One steady the far rail. Others go in. Once in, stay afloat an' bail."

We feared the craft rode too low an' we'd lose her. Yet the shark left no choice. She held as we half lifted each other in. Captain, an' the three more eased in last. Four bailed as we helped the last in. Last a seven that was, all but the one steadying the boat. Sadly, as we reached ta grab 'im, that man with his broke arm got pulled under, sudden an' silent, no splash.

Just so quick we were seven.

(II) Aboard the Smallboat

(19) We're out, afloat, an' battered

With four kegs hard bailing, we cleared out much a the boat's water till she rode high. We'd rescued the foundering craft, all the while praying she'd return the favor.

We headed out ta scavenge the wreckage. Two men used kegs as paddles, whilst two still bailed.

"Carefull not ta step in the breach, men. Tear the tarp, an' we're lost," Captain warned. "Ya men paddling, don't get hands down wet if ya prefer owning ten fingers."

I doubt any needed that word. We clearly saw the sharks swimming so frightfully near, cold saucer eyes staring up.

'Twas nearing eve. First need in the flotsam was oars. We found four ship's oars, long for this boat, yet they fit the powlocks, an' could be used as is, till we'd shorten the handles.

The oars, moved us quick ta the kegs the men'd pushed out a the *Vengeferth*. Eight small ones soon filled the stern, each lined ta a large one afloat. We were pulling 'em in ta take off clothes wrapped on, then pushing the kegs back out still tied on. A pile a clothing grew in the middle a the boat.

Lit by a near full moon, Captain wound lines on the kegs attached ta us 'round the lines a more kegs. He kept out an eye for sharks, whilst endangering his hands as he'd warned us against. They twice came nipping up like teased pups jumping for a treat, but he flinched back an inch quick enough each time. One came up far enough ta show his hammer's head.

I watched a time, weary an' unable ta move. Done in, I nested in two coats an' a slicker there in the bow. Soon my sorely aching body found the great gentle comfort a sleep.

Even much banging a nails failed ta bother my heavy sleep. Our tireless Captain used Cookie's meat hammer, an' nails from men's pockets ta secure the sail we'd wrapped under our boat. He rolled the edges an' nailed 'em just below inside the rail all 'round. Whilst he did that, others sorted from the flotsam a right sized board ta cover the breach in the hull. Now no man half-asleep would step through an' sink the boat.

Evidence a all that work was much encouragement when half the sun on the horizon woke me. I raised my head an' studied the scene, feeling pain an' soreness with each move. I deep breathed honey sweet air. Everything considered, *all* wasn't honey sweet. 'Twas sweet we had a usable boat 'neath us. Sweet we had kegs a food an' water ta survive a time. Sweet that much material lay strewn about, awaiting our use. Most sweet 'twas that we, breathing, flesh an' blood men, had met a most tremendous wall an' were wondrously no crumbs brushed ta the floor. Yet a storm was abrew on the horizon.

Factually, *there she was! A* squall looming at us from the north. I espied her, though she half hid behind our desperate, low sinking Vengeferth, struggling still, like a whale last-gasping. I rousted the men, whilst beseeching: W*hen might we lowly men expect ta draw a peacefull breath in this bloody lifetime?*

Captain awoke, followed my gaze ta the squall, an' directed straight out, "Drink water, men. We'll eat whilst she rains. Two men lash better the kegs afloat. We need masts lashed port an' starb'rd. Yardarms cross 'em fore an' aft, if we've time. Tarp o'er the top, an' we'll sit safe as ducks."

'Twas assembled fast. Lash a mast ta the left. Then row through flotsam ta a mast for the right. Me an' Doc worked securing a tarp atop. The chop picked up, growing the work harder. 'Twas going nighttime dark at mid morn. Yet they lashed yardarms, bow an' stern, across the masts. 'Twas finished as showers turned ta coming down in bucketfulls.

She tore at us wild. Bounced us like biscuits in a barrel. Were we safe as ducks, I'd plead the Captain find a far different animal next storm out. Our *Vengeferth* seemed a bobber in a squall, yet 'twas a fine comfort beside this crazy throw around.

We clasped seats much the way we'd hugged bed legs, it seemed so long ago, riding out the monster wall. The difference was that the wall went just so quick, an' this seemed ta never end, never end, never end, a whole *hun*dred never ends, an' yet countless *more* never ends. Yet it did end quite sudden. Did so without us hanging worrisomely upside down. We rode it through mostly hanging sideways, yet ended topside up.

We sat stunned. Bruises an' batters, piled upon the bruises an' batters a the day 'fore. Pain atop pain o'er wound upon welt. Seemed the monster wall'd come through ages ago, but only in the mind, not in every mercy-beggin muscle a the body. I was pulp. Bloody beaten ta pulp. Seemed Cookie'd worked me tender with his meat hammer. The chop was down, the sun sinking, an' I was dog hungry, but willing only ta nest in the bow amongst clothes, an' fall again gladly inta the lovely waiting arms a sleep. None stirred. We were all pulp.

(20) The seven

We were seven aboard a speck a flotsam on the vast ocean, Captain, Doc, Heitman, Dessinger, Gorden, Reed, an' me.

First there's Captain. O'er six foot, salt-an-pepper bearded, an' large nosed. Yet only ta passersby. Know 'im a minute, an' the protrusion goes forgot. I say salt an' pepper on the beard, yet the salt is sparse, an' he keeps it yet more trim than my own, not long an' willy-nilly. No belly rug, rat's nest.

Ya seen already his fine, strong nature. Y'll see more.

He's no dandy man. A low dresser, yet wearing his bold hats. Favors the o'ersized brim, yet not big plumed nor bejeweled. Aye wide-brims. Seems the brim's ta shade the nose. He eschews the fancy garb many Captains flaunt. (*Eschews?* Gesundheit. Such fun, the rarer word well spent. My pardon.)

Doc is Captain's chess mate. They're Pat an' Mike. Captain tall an' daring, Doc the short thinker. Early on they whittled chess pieces from debris an' carved a board at the center a their aft bench. Ya could find 'em there. A' times I took on the winner. I could push 'em, yet they'd thump me eight in ten.

Doc's short, with muscles he exercised daily on the *Vengeferth's* deck. The scientist, he wears a smooth face, an' trim mustache. His razor went down with the ship, so his beard was soon revealed. 'Twas, as his hair, sandy brown.

Doc also was our handyman. Had tools ta fix anything. He's the kindest disposed man I know, an' I'd swear it down ta the ground, were he editing this tome or no. *(Editor Doc insists he's imperfect. Mayhap, yet I'm well fooled.)*

Yet Jamie Gorden owns a kind disposition as well. A puzzle. He oft talks slow an' thoughtfull, yet moves quick an' easy. Still owns smithing muscles. Years ahead a 'imself. Y'd think 'im on religion's path, yet he *eschews* the church.

Young Dessinger an' Heitman grew ta be brothers. Close partners, but I doubt a Jonesy an' Willie B's bent. Yet ya don't know. Naught does it matter. Both slim, young, an' full a life. They laugh easy. Heitman's the taller an' stronger. Dessinger sings like an angel an' worked the riggin easy as a dance.

Reed was the seventh man. 'Twas his first voyage out. Red-headed, with all the skin frecks that come with a carrot top. Youngest an' sparsest built. His fiery hair was long, yet only half the length a Gorden's shoulder-covering blond locks.

It should be mind-numbing for a man, first time out, ta find such huge piles a confusion, an' craziness. None'd be surprised were Reed wild eyed an' all ashake. Yet he seemed the least disheveled, taking all in stride. I saw 'im as still of a childish mind. He'd played child's pirate games. Must a come 'board seeking adventure, an' found all as expected. Should he stay a' sea, he'd surely find his days yawnfully repetitive. Likely leave behind the seafaring life due ta boredom.

I was the old man. A whit grizzled. Past my prime. Eyes a bit bleary at a distance, but not bad close up for reading. Teeth starting ta go. Ears fine though. I'd turned a half century. I brought experience aboard. Seen enough ta know a little more. Still got around pretty good when I had ta.

(21) Getting organized

Hid in darkness by our fine canvas roof, I slept till noon. Swear I could a slept through another night, or even two, but for nature's call. The anger a my vacant belly was growing intolerable as well, an' it began ta rumble loud. Sore an' painfull, I stuck up my head. I knew the feel of a well kicked cur.

Whilst' tending nature's needs, I cast an eye about the horizon. Finding no squalls, huge walls or other disasters jumping themselves up, I considered our condition. Masts lashed port an' starb'rd, an' yardarms fore an' aft had all stayed firm. Well held by good line, they'd kept us aright. I'd had some doubts there, yet was too wrung out ta fret. Sail cover we'd hastened ta tie down held tight as well. Saying she kept us dry'd be a stretch, yet we were far from drowned. Two barrels 'd bounced off the stern, an' one inside smashed. Pickle brine smell brought sad memories a slogging in the dank *Vengeferth*.

Speaking a her, our valiant *Vengeferth* was gone. Squall 'd put her down. She gave sadly up, an' went ta spend forever on the murky bottom. A saddest amen ta her. Unfortunately for us, the storm'd swept the debris as well. The wide blue ocean 'twas clean as far as the eye could see. Flotsam we could a used ta improve our condition was strewn beyond sight. Or had it stayed where 'twas whilst we scattered far distant?

"G'morn, Mister DeVoe," Captain Werthman spoke soft, yet startling, as he sidled up aside me. "'Tis sad ta see we lost the debris we hoped ta use. I had such plans ta put boards across the two masts in back till we had a floor where we'd stretch our legs, an' could store the kegs. Ah well, plans oft go for naught. All we have looks fine, but for a few kegs. Some are leaking. We'd best bring 'em in 'fore the sharks get interested an' tear inta 'em. Then we'll eat morn mess an' figure what ta do."

"Aye, Captain, g'morn," I grumbled. "Guess we must move, though these weary bones protest at lifting a pinky finger."

"Aye, rest's what our wrung out bodies beg, but we can't give the sharks our food. A long, hungry time may face us."

We turned ta lading kegs aboard. Soon the others were helping. Some hauled 'em in, others lashed 'em atop the masts an' yardarms 'round the boat. All told, we had twenty-eight barrels a food, an' eight kegs a water about us. Far too many ta carry in the boat. We soon sat amid a floating feast table. Seven kegs yet left inside were too many. Captain opened two kegs, one salt pork, the other mixed nuts, shelled. We sat an' filled our famished selves, resting our tortured bodies.

Captain talked whilst passing out the salt pork. "Fill your bellies, but don't go pig just 'cause we've so much. No telling how long this food must last. Better ta eat less now an' not starve later. Same for water. Don't o'erdrink. An' keep shaded, so's not ta be sweating it out so quick.

"We're in fine shape," Captain went on. "All beat ta putty, but without serious injury. The broke wrist we had went down with Jim Horner, taken by a shark. Doc, how about a prayer for 'im, lost steadying the boat as we eased in. He's owed our lives."

Doc gave a strong prayer. Told how sad we were, an' thankfull ta the brave soul who stayed in the water steadying the boat just a tad too long. He went on ta speak low a friends who went so sadly down in the *Vengeferth,* as well as the unfortunates aboard the *Daisy Belle.* An' he spoke on poor Willie B who we tried ta do our best by, yet put on the wrong ship ta have a chance. Doc gave our goodbyes ta the swift, strong *Vengeferth* herself. She'd carried us safe an' sheltered through many a storm. Then, in her finest hour, she struggled us finally through the ocean's greatest challenge, just ta find herself wrong side up an' lost. Was no dry eye aboard.

We went about the afternoon most quiet. Captain used spare wood ta fashion a powlock inta the aft rail, so one shortened oar gave us a rudder. Whilst he did that, me, Doc, an' Gorden secured two a the long oars ta the boat's back corners, aimed upwards. Near their tops, we made holes an' tied on two corners a our cover tarp. We tied on the tarp's other two corners ta the rail by the bow. Thus we'd fashioned a fine sail ta funnel the wind through from the rear o'er our heads. It had most excellent bonuses, in that it shaded us from the sun much a the day an' aimed down ta us some breeze as well.

We busied ourselves moving food amongst kegs. Aboard ship we'd reduced all ta near half full. We now refilled 'em ta three quarters, thus leaving some empty. Candle wax resealed 'em. Captain wedged a small keg 'neath the seat ta hold down the board o'er the hull's breach. Empties we lashed astern.

(22) The Captain explains, then charges me

We were sorely thankfull for a fair weather day at last. Late mess found our craft in good shape. Stiff an' painfull, we ate salt pork an' nuts, casting eyes on the fruits a our labor.

"Captain, what was the meaning of the cannon blasts we heard whilst tightening ship?" Doc asked, as Captain handed out salt pork. "Were you trying to shoot the monster wall down? Or did it just seem a fine day for target practice?"

"What he did," I put in, "was first clear away half the bottom main yardarm. Second shot hit the main mast. 'Twent ta starb'rd taking out the rail. I thought y'd gone soft in the head at the time, sir, but there sure was no arguing with ya. What the devil was your bloody thinking on that, Captain?"

"I know ya men think your Captain spends all his livelong days in his quarters beating up poor Doc here in chess. On the rarest occasion losing. (He paused as we chuckled.) But I spend hours mulling o'er the course a action in situations. A' times I pondered the wall. The monster rumored ta come charging most disastrously through ever so seldom. We seven now know for dead certain she's no fiction nor exaggeration."

Heads nodded, swear words were muttered, an' he went on, "It seemed best were we evenly balanced an' light. Heaviest weight aboard was cannons. No way ta rid us a the lower guns, yet their weight was spread even, ta the four corners.

"Both deck guns ta the front made for an unbalanced ship. Clearing those guns'd lighten ship an' even out the weight."

"How'd ya clear 'em o'er the side so quick?" Reed asked.

"We unlocked the cleats, spun 'em, an' the kickback did it."

"But," I asked, "why'd we shoot out the main mast?"

"Aye, I'd lost sleep a' times pondering it. Shooting guns just ta clear 'em seemed a waste. Yet with no main mast, we'd be lighter an' more stable. Blown straight on, the mast'd hit the mizzenmast, fall full on the deck, an' surely bust it. So I unbalanced her by half a yardarm, then the second shot sent her off starb'rd, not breaking up the deck. 'Twent fine, yet was of no avail in the end. Alas, our *Vengeferth* flipped an' went lost."

"Got it right enough ta save seven lives," Gorden avowed.

"Aye," Captain nodded.

"We beat a wall, sir," Reed declared, "What's more proof?"

"It seems," Captain agreed. "But Doc, why'd we lose so many men? What can ya see as causing the death a so many?"

"She went up like a high breaching whale," Doc answered. "The men by the bow went high and fell far, crashing down with great force. Their heads must have bounced sorely hard. The stern may have not even cleared the water, so men aboard there, fell little distance. Most survivors were to the stern. We were lucky she was a strong ship, or we'd all have perished."

"Wall was a real nutcracker," I observed, chewing salt pork. "Didn't break our *Vengeferth's* hull, but busted many a skull."

"That's about it," Doc nodded. "But it ended quick. For us, as well as the poor souls we lost. Unlike the squall that kept going forever. Aboard this tiny craft forever is a long time."

"Aye," Captain nodded. "Coming on us, she appeared small. Just went on kicking us down the road. I've bruises I'll be long feeling. Yet at least we've confidence this smallboat can weather a bad one. We'll not meet worse 'n that."

"'Tis certain we learned how popping corn feels," I jested.

Captain's eyes widened, as did his smile. He gave a guffaw that sprayed half-chewed food. We all turned ta laughing. Layed out guffawing an' rolling, though it reawoke much pain an' countless bruises. We laughed ourselves tearfull eyed, an' Dessinger did some small choking on salt pork.

Being in a humorous bent, my head jumped ta another quip. I giggled it out, "We should a been military, Captain, being as we bounced about like so many kernels."

We lay an' laughed ourselves out. Went on till we grew weak as kittens. Looking back, it seems there was more in it than my jests. We were laughing out the built up pain of strong sadness deep inside from the loss a dear friends who went down with our *Vengeferth*. Laughter, such fine, needed medication.

"Devoe, ya missed your calling, ya pip," Captain gasped, mid recapturing his breath. "Ya could best the king's jester any day an' aught ta own his job. Y've a gift a words, an' when your two feet stand ashore, *I **charge ya*** with finding a day ta put pen ta paper an' tell the tale a this crazy trip we near ending. It'll fill a book ta support ya in retirement. I look for'rd much ta reading it. We've out adventured Caruso an' Gulliver together. Ya needn't change our tribulations a whit. Though," he chuckled, "subtracting slightly from the nose wouldn't hurt."

"Ah, a little off the nose," I pondered, putting up my thumb, as though measuring ta carve his bust.

"No, leave it. 'Twas Lord assigned. I'll not second guess 'im."

Our Captain, a rugged, handsome bloke, despite his de Bergerac nose, offered up a fine idea. I'm hopefull he got it mostly right. Particularly the retiring part. Yet he missed the mark measuring our trip near its end. Tiresome days lie ahead.

(23) The first days

Bodies an' minds were wrung out. Those days a chaos had seemed months in passing, like uninvited, down-an'-out relatives. Stinking nasty ones. We took the beating well though. Yet Heitman stayed thrown off 'imself awhile. Jumpy-eyed, he flung his next glance oft ta the horizon. A tensed up cur preparing ta flinch. Ready for the next boot kick. But he, as well, came aright in a few days.

All shared life's purest joy at being so lucky ta emerge from death's shadow. That joy cheered us from our body's pain a countless bruises, an' our soul's pain a lost friends. We lay about, tasting sweet our every breath an' soaking deep the suns pouring warmth. We were well alive aboard a sturdy enough craft with much food an' water, whilst bruises faded an' we grew back our strength a body. Steadily our strength a mind returned as well. Yet battering a the mind is slower ta fade. A' times I had night visions a lost friends floating about my feet as I slogged through a murky *Vengeferth*. Others awoke sweaty as well, calling out, clearly having beheld ugly pictures.

One night we woke ta cries an' thrashing. 'Twas Heitman wrestling a creature in his mind. 'Fore he could be grabbed, he stood an' pitched o'er the side. Water cold on his face woke 'im. We fished 'im out quick. Lucky no shark slept 'neath us. I've heard they do that, hanging about dreaming on a tasty treat. I worried a shark's knife top fin might cut the sail wrapping our birthday present boat. We'd be that shark's gift.

So 'twas. Nights oft nasty, an' days dozing in an' out, laying about, happy down ta our toes at being alive.

Our handy sail moved us along. It even found another welcome an' expected use one morn, when an easy shower came o'er. Many kegs set 'neath the sail's waiting edge were filled by sweet runoff. We felt so refreshed ta stand face ta the heavens an' bathe in unbriny sweetwater's purest sweetness.

I say the sail worked fine, yet she had problems. With masts lashed ta our sides, she took us only with the breeze any way it decided. By lowering one back corner a the sail an' using our makeshift rudder, we could vary some small degree off the wind, but we slowed. An' ta say the sail ever clipped us along is a stretch. A fast crawl at best. Parting ways with the masts an' yardarms lashed about would increase our speed an' we'd steer better, but we couldn't face a squall without 'em steadying us, nor could we lug all our kegs. Later on we lashed more heavy water kegs atop the mast parts behind, nosed the bow up some, an' gained a bit a speed. But our pace lagged. Yet 'tis hard ta gauge ones speed on a vastness a ocean.

(24) Our situation

Being creatures a habit, as all creatures find comfort in habit, we each grew inta the seats we took earliest on. Quickest ta tire that first eve, I'd retreated inta sleep farthest out a the way, curled up in the smaller bow bench. Much later Captain an' Doc parked at ends a the stern seat. Heitman an' Dessinger took the next seat, whilst Reed an' Gorden claimed that nearest me. We had ta curl up ta sleep. Near fifteen foot stem ta stern, an' just o'er six foot across, the boat allowed no stretching. We'd a slept more men, were it necessary, yet selfishly liked the modest sleeping space our number allowed.

I'd oft complained in silence at the cramped quarters on our Vengeferth. Now a man's space was tiny, yet I appreciated my spared life such that I never grumbled why our smallboat's maker didn't add another inch. 'Twas tight, yet our one chance. That close space may a been good. Wouldn't allow us ta separate an' drift off alone. The small area forced us ta stay more together. None could recede ta a corner in his mind.

Twixt seats, lines stretched, rail ta rail. Those lines lashed the masts ta either side an' went under the boat. We wrapped 'em many times about each mast, ta cushion 'em against banging the boat an' tearing the tarp wrapped under us. Lines across were an awkward nuisances tripping ya up a' times. Yet in a high chop they were handy for steadying yourself.

The masts ta each side went out far longer 'n the boat. For balance we evened 'em for'rd an' aft. Yardarms, lashed atop the masts, bow an' stern, went wide as well, yet were shorter 'n the masts. We jawed a' times on removing the front yardarm ta gain some small speed, but feared for our craft in a squall, an' let well enough alone. An error might be fatal, as clearly we couldn't quickly redo anything we undid.

So that's how we were riding. Had there been a bird about, ta look down, he might a taken us for a game a Naughts an' Crosses. We being a naught in the middle. As days wore farther along, we felt more an' more the nearest ta naught.

(25) We fashion a sea anchor

A week on, Captain spoke up at morn mess, "Men, we've been bone idle a time. Healing our battered bodies after a fierce ordeal was the only thing ta do, but now 'tis time ta pick ourselves up an' go about planning this trip."

"In many ways we're in an encouraging situation, men. We're 'board a small craft with a breached hull, yet she feels good. She's storm tested an' likely ta stay afloat a good while.

Our food supply is fine. We'll eat well for a time. Won't sit still an rot, moved along by this sail. She offers fine shade, an' she'll give us good runoff ta fill many kegs when it rains.

"Ta the poor side, the wall's swept the sea clean a ships we could find. Yet we're moving on. Might spot an island tomorrow, or a continent next week. All's likely, yet organized, we'll have a better chance a getting through alive. 'Tis true no matter where we go or how long we take getting there."

"Can ya plot the stars on a clear night, Captain, an' fathom where on this earth we sit?" Reed asked.

"No, not hardly. Doc has the scientific mind here, an' neither can he manage that without the maps an' tools on my desk that went down with the *Vengeferth*. I can only tell fairly close our distance from the equator. A man who knows the season a the year, can gauge the height a the north star off the horizon an' glean his distance north an' south on this planet. It takes no instruments or Copernicus ta figure. Sun's height at noon'll give fair estimation too, but 'tis hard ta gauge in a tiny boat, even when there's no chop. Yet ta fathom even near his position east ta west, a man needs the maps an' tools.

"'Tis a puzzlement why we're being pushed along by wind from the east. Most times ships heading west in these parts are slowed 'cause they must work inta eastward flowing headwind. Our vessel, using this sail, can't come near working inta the wind. Most we can vary 's about fifteen degrees off the wind, an' that slows us. Also, we must be carefull not ta break the oars holding up the sail. She gets blowing hard, an' we must lower the sail some. We're headed west with the wind, varying south as best we can. Last place we need ta go is north an' freeze. Should we catch a hard northbound breeze, we'll pull down the sail an' put out a sea anchor."

"Did we bring a sea anchor, Captain? This water seems mighty deep," Reed asked, showing a landlubber's innocence, an' bringing snickers an' guffaws.

"No, Mister Reed. Sea anchors don't resemble what you're thinking. We'll fashion one from an empty keg. Y'll see what they're about. Pay no mind ta the laughter. I've seen no recruit come aboard with knowledge a sea anchors an' such.

"When I was a raw recruit, an old salt had me believing we had a rubber stretching line aboard ship. It would stretch ta the bottom with a sea anchor at its end. He sent me on a fool's errand around the ship, asking who had the stretch line for the sea anchor. 'Tis an o'er worn jest a' seamen.

"I'm charging Mister DeVoe with carving a keg inta a sea anchor 'fore dusk. He'll show ya, Mister Reed, how one's made an' used. Long 'fore eve y'll see the humor in your question.

"Now, I want ta tell about exercises we can do aboard this tiny boat an' need ta do quite regular."

Captain set out ways ta exercise. I must say they were excellent, as was their purpose, ta keep our muscles fit an' have us burn off energy, yet their description is even a tad more boring than the exercises themselves, an' I swore ta cull such tiresome, boring stuff from this story.

His exercises were about lifting kegs an' other busyness. Manning the oars was another idea. 'Twas all fine stuff, if so unenjoyable. I admit that doing it left one feeling good. Yet banging one's head on a wall, feels good after ya stop.

"All we need ta fashion a sea anchor," I soon was explaining ta Reed, "is a dagger, an empty keg, this hammer an' one nail. It takes a short time. We cut a sizable hole in the bottom a the keg, put a nail by the top, an' there ya be.

"A sea anchor's just something dragged along ta slow ya when the wind wants ta send ya in the wrong direction. She'll also steady a craft some in a squall. The masts lashed ta either side slow us no matter which way we go, an' steady us in a squall, but any bit can make some difference. Sea anchor'll keep us facing inta the wind whilst we sleep. When you're fighting a headwind, straight on is the way ta stay steady."

Reed was a quick learn. Yet 'tis no deep science. A boat drags a keg ta slow her. Yet there's a finer point on it. Ya must know the right way ta line up the hole in the bucket's bottom an' the nail in the side, so she'll stay down an' steady, not float an' bob as wood wants ta do.

"Are sea anchors used 'board the ships?" Reed asked.

"Seldom. Trim her sails right, an' a ship'll zig zag inta the wind at a good clip. A ship may use a canvas sea anchor nights when the crew needs rest, an' faces a strong headwind."

(26) The boring stuff

Days began ta pile atop days, with small change or excitement. They grew themselves longer each by each, bit by bit.

Back on the second day, Captain had pulled out hooks an' line he carried many years sewn in his waistcoat for emergencies. So we were able ta catch fish an' add 'em ta our diet.

Raw fish is healthy food, yet all owns a same tiresome flavor. A flavor that grows less inviting bite by bite. We oft had the problem a bigger sharks on the line. Smaller ones we ate. From big ones we just asked our hook an' line back. Didn't want 'em aboard eating us 'fore we could eat 'em. A dagger tied ta an oar could make a passable spear ta kill 'em, but we worried about losing one a only two daggers we owned. Oars were also precious items. So we waited till the shark's razor teeth cut the hook off. We had many nails ta bend inta hooks, yet each time our fish line worrysomely shrunk shorter.

Days were boredom, exercise, boredom, doze in an' out a sleep, boredom, catch a fish, doze in an' out a sleep, play some chess, more boredom, an' more boredom. Boredom an' uncertainty wore on us. Uncertainty was low mumbling thunder on the horizon, ever bothersome.

My apology. I broke my vow ta leave out all the humdrum boring, put-ya-ta-sleep stuff, but in the seventh week I asked Captain Werthman about how he came by his six magical cannons. From there on, eves after mess turned ta story time.

"Captain," I started, as he doled out shark meat, "if I'm ta put this adventure ta the page, as ya charged, it seems ya missmeasured. Our voyage began fierce, yet the craziness was a few days. I'll need a hefty book ta allow comfort in my old age, a comfort well deserved after the wearing down a this crazy trip.

Should I spend ink on the lengthy boredom we're now enduring, 'twill bore readers ta sleep, likely even ta tears. I'll need more excitement ta pour ta the page. Tell about how ya came by those magical guns we sadly lost aboard the *Vengeferth*."

I'd been first mate on the *Vengeferth* four trips an' knew little a his storied cannons. He seldom spoke on 'em. The guns' magical accuracy 'd grown in mystery among the drinking holes aport, where sailors jaw loud an' swill away money.

Aboard our *Vengeferth* the cannons were spoke of in hushed tones. I had few clues on where they came from, nor the secrets a their amazing workings. Captain'd mentioned a few words about his brother an 'im building 'em, but he never went on. I hoped ta wheedle his secrets in detail for this tome, which a' times I was uncertain I'd live ta pen.

(27) Captain's first trip

"The tale a my misspent youth lacks excitement. I'll tell ya a my first trip out as Captain. 'Tis a far more stirring tale.

"'Twasn't so long ago," he started in, "though, like this trip's start, it seems distant. The crew was good, yet rowdy. My recruiting eye was unpracticed. I could mistake bluster for skill.

"I'd sailed a two year tour, then been a' land two, yet never a' sea as a ship's Captain. So I stayed quiet, playing the Captain roll, wise an' confident, as the men need. I had ta choose carefull the first boat we took. Too big 'd be bad, an' military a disaster. Poor immigrants 'd do us little good, an' I'd look the fool. Second ship we espied was a sizable pirate vessel with near three times our crew. Wanted nothing ta do with 'em, but they insisted ta fight. The bullies expected ta have fun taking us. We sorely quaked at what the ruffians planned if they did.

"We'd outrun 'em, but it could be a close race if their hull was clean. They had all their canvas up. Turning tail meant having but our stern guns ta use, guns a tad less accurate with both ships running full bore in the same direction.

"They came straight on portside nearing gun range. I had ta swiftly decide, an' did so, hearing worry in my crew when I gave oarsmen orders ta turn an' face 'em. I raised our battle flag, an' checked with the gunners that the guns were loaded an' ready. My spyglass was prepared ta set the guns' aim. I was asweat right down ta the deck. I'd practiced my shooting, but 'twas a far different arena here. This was do or die. We'd need two quick hits out a four. Should we miss, she'd veer off an' pass us broad-side, too near ta miss. Then we'd show a white flag, an' be at their mercy. Their mercy appeared in short supply.

"But our guns worked like a lucky charm. Our first shot took down her main mast, an' the second sheared her mizzen mast. She had some small momentum left. I had the oarsmen back us ta the edge a gun range whilst we pulled down the battle flag an' reraised her upside down. Ta Reed I explain that an upside down battle flags says 'tis your last chance, all's done, surrender now, else you're going down.

"Dead in the water, an' having seen amazing gun work, she quick raised a white flag. My crew cheered. We righted our battle flag, an' sat back awaiting her Captain as our guest.

"Yet they were clearly a the bullying sort. Trickery might still be their game. Skullduggery'd be less likely should their Captain came out quick. He took some time getting started o'er, thus getting hairs on my neck prickled.

"Then came a whaling boat, four ta the oars an' the Captain. A smallboat was in tow. We were ta expect the smallboat had loot. I liked it the least. All pirates know only a Captain an' two ta the oars come across in a smallboat. They stay as hostage guests, whilst our gang goes out ta rummage their ship.

"We winched down a smallboat, an' put our flag upside down. Thus telling the Captain in his whaleboat I was unhappy. I urged the six we sent out ta be carefull. Show us a red flag at trouble's first sign. They went armed with pistols an' swords.

"Our cannons were reloaded, two lined up on her waterline an' one on each boat coming across. As our smallboat neared 'em, I saw in my eyeglass, four men rise up in the smallboat, muskets drawn. The five in the bigger front boat became suddenly ten, all with drawn muskets as well. As was clearly planned, all their big cannons then fired on us. Our men out there fell quickly ta the smallboat's floor. We fired on their two boats. Then we fired twice on their ship's water line.

"Being as we were on the edge a gunning range, only one a their poorly aimed balls came near us. Whilst our four shots hit every target. Both smallboats blew inta toothpicks, an' two holes showed at their waterline. Our smallboat had one dead, two wounded, an' three fine. Those wounded, well survived. Our smallboat was full a holes an' sinking.

"Ta speak a sinking, holes at her waterline (bow, both sides) put her down in an hour. I muttered as she sunk. 'Twas no apology. Men in smallboats headed our way, but I didn't trust the treacherous cutthroats near us. Nor had we room for 'em.

"Very least did we want their muddle brained Captain 'board. He wasn't half sharp enough ta be dull. Clearly he'd stayed 'board ship an' sent a man dressed in his garb. Clad as a minion, the fool 'd now hide 'board a smallboat, a pistol in his boot. We pushed off a smallboat with fish line an' hooks an' set sail.

"Nothing's gained sinking ships. Putting rich folks' trinkets in our pocket is fun. Seeing valuables sink is a sad waste. Ships sent sailing home might one day float back ta refill our locker.

"What'd that muddleheaded Captain think? Stupid pride wasted 'im a ship. Yet he espied but four small guns aimed at 'im. Perhaps he was a the mind that he'd lost his masts ta lucky shots. Even were they good luck shots, seems the bloody fool might a fathomed 'twas not his lucky day.

(28) Gorden's interrupted

Telling each other stories made the live-long days more tolerable aboard the *Vengeferth*. We'd turned a' times ta calling our craft *Vengeferth*, being as 'twas her smallboat, an' the masts an' yardarms about us were a the beautyfull ship as well. Feelings for the mother ship we'd always liked, clearly grew as we tired more an' more in our mindwearing situation.

We agreed ta take turns telling stories on happenings in our lives after eve mess. Stories picked up our spirits, yet we couldn't tell tales all day. We had all the time, but lacked tales in such numbers. Stories continuously told, we also knew, would take on a dronesome boredom a their own. Captain had more exciting tales ta tell than we others taken together, so he was charged with having a turn every other eve. After some few protestations, he agreed.

Next night Gorden drew short straw. Chop was up an' the breeze cool. After eve mess we tied down our cover tarp an', for the first time, heaved our sea anchor off the bow ta add an ounce ta the boat's steadiness. We'd bailed every drop a loose water ta be found. Each nested in slickers an' all the dry clothing items we had about, giving us warm, dry comfort.

"I've been a' sea but a single trip 'fore this," Gorden started. "All a ya but Reed know what I've seen a' sea. So I'll go back ta my youth. There was little excitement in my upbringing. I'll keep it short. Half a ya are likely ta snore 'fore I finish."

A bloke snorted in the darkness. Some chuckled.

"Wait a minute. I wasn't even born yet," he chided.

"Ya might skip the being born," was said, adding chuckles.

"Men," came the Captain, in laughter, "ya best let 'im start, else he'll ne'er reach the end an' we'll be here all night."

"What do you mind if he takes all night, Captain?" came Doc's smiling voice. "Have you a cozy appointment with a comely lass you expect to soon hurry off to, yourself?"

Guffaws came an' quieted, till Gorden started back, "So I was young an' small. As requested, I'll pass by life's first minutes. Memory being a bit foggy in that area. I've been told I was heard ta gowl some."

"Well heard?" I asked.

"Aye, well heard," he laughed. "I had strong lungs."

"Heard far an' wide I suspect," I slipped in.

"Aye far an' wide!" he snapped, feigning impatience.

"Strong lungs indeed. 'Tis proved out," I chuckled.

At that point in our banter, we suddenly lurched strong. Laughter cut ta silence. We sat trying ta fathom the cause. My mind was jerked back ta seeing the frailty in our situation.

"What's your take, Captain?" came whispered in the dark.

'Fore the question was answered, another jolt. Different this time, less sudden, yet tugging the boat for'rd a short bit.

"A sizable shark fancies the sea anchor," Captain said.

His dagger whispered, clearing its scabbard.

"Wil, take my knife. Pull in the line. If she fights ya, cut the line. No value in a keg, but it'd be good ta save as much line as ya safely can. Be sure ta bring back all ten fingers."

I tucked the dagger in my belt. Fumbling with the tarp cover took time. 'Twas well tied down, an' the chop kept me wobbly. Out from under, I reached for the line, an' the beast yanked. I fell back. It gave the feel she'd soon wrench our smallboat asunder. I clambered back up an' grabbed it. The line came in easy with the keg on. Near the boat, that keg got seized hard. Line racing out lit my palms afire 'fore I could let go. The boat pitched, an' I reflexed, clutching rail. Fire in my hands put tears ta my eyes. This jolt felt so near tearing the boat apart.

I'd been nearly tossed a' sea. Alas, I turned the dagger ta sawing through the line, whilst fiercely spitting foul language at the beast an' at the fire in my palms. An' then the rope went clear. Amen. Yet captain's dagger slid from my blood-slippery grasp as the line went aloose. I ducked back in.

"A jerk came as I reeled in," I shrilled through the huge burn a my palms, "an' the line tore my hands deep. Then I cut the line, but as it sawed through, from my bloody hand slipped the dagger an' went lost."

"'Tis much my fault," Captain moaned. "I shouldn't a given a fools thought ta saving the damn line."

Relief at being rid a the beast, piled atop angry fire burning my palms, an' the strong worry a losing the dagger. All came pouring o'er an' put me ta sobbing like a small baby.

Captain wordlessly sat hugging tight my strong shaking, whilst behind the Captain's back', Doc wrapped cloth around my burning palms. He held me long after, till my shakes calmed. Throbs a my hands allowed little sleep that night.

(29) Half a Gorden's story

    Why a simple truth snuck past us seven geniuses is a mystery. "Twas easy ta see that the keg held a whiff a foodstuffs lingering deep. Some odors are small, but generous Mother Nature gave sharks the biggest noses. "Even bigger 'n mine," our good Captain chuckled. 'Tis claimed they can whiff blood in the water miles away." No more thoughts a sea anchors.

  Next morn, an' for many days, they fed me like a baby. My angry palms rested. Did nothing. Not that something needed doing those long days. Calls a nature I managed.

   Two hours daily, Doc's soaked my hands in sweetwater, bringing back the hot pain an' my foul words. With much apology, Doc insisted. I knew he had it right, yet kept wishing he'd forget a whit longer. 'Twas a too small boat. I couldn't flee nor shrivel up an' hide. For the moment I disliked the site a 'im.

   Later, with healed hands, I offered regret ta Doc for sadly letting my pain bring on such words an' vilify 'im, the kindest soul aboard. He gave a guffaw on my words, an' soon I joined in his good laughter. Doc, a deep friend a fine wisdom.

  'The day after my hands were hurt, Captain an' Gorden had a competition. They chose large nails ta fashion inta knives. Each trying ta better the other. The last true dagger aboard was tied on in the stern. They took turns carving their new knife handles with that dagger. Their handles were fine, an' fit together well with each nail, but they couldn't get their nails filed near blade sharp. The points were sharp though, so they weren't useless. We a' times used one on an oar ta gaff sharks.

   That eve, after mess, Gorden went back ta telling his story. We again nested in the darkness beneath our tied down roof. The wind stayed cold, an' the chop ran high.

  "Where was I when the rude fish disrupted?" Gorden asked.

  "Ya told a being a scrawny runt with strong lungs. Blubbered so long an' loud the folks oft considered strangling ya," Came Reed's smiling voice. "The shark cut ya off where they were getting few blinks a sleep day an' night, as were the neighbors."

  "Aye," Gorden laughed, "so I'll skip o'er that part.

"I grew bigger, day by day, bit by bit. Till I got past being a gowling runt. I grew inta a normal older child."

"A bigger one," Reed stated.

"Yep, a truly bigger one a normal size. Yet never so big as my big sister for a time. Rosie kept on being older an' always bigger. A course she teased me, as all older sisters are expected ta continually do. Yet we became friends. At least many days we were. Till I finally outgrew her in size. Then we both teased each other, an' I saw what great fun 'twas both ways. We went on ta be the best friends.

In a more serious voice he went on, "My folks were fine, good people. Dad clanging away smithing in the shop by the road, Mom raisin fine chickens an' a garden full a vegetables an' fruit. She cooked up great smells as well, an' sang most sweetly away the sweet days. The time a harvesting, preserving, an' making fruit jams was my favorite. Work much enjoyed.

Rosie an' me helped her till I grew up enough ta help Dad smithing. Then me an' Dad helped the girls a' times with the heavier lifting. We kids both went years ta school, helping out at home as well. I did better at learning smithing than book learning. Dad was the better teacher. Yet I did pick up my letters an' numbers, growing nearly as good as Rosie.

"A shadow came o'er our lives when the fever took Mom. She was sick a time, yet it seemed fast. She was abed a few weeks, yet quietly, such that it seemed she might be healing.

"After that sadness, Rosie quit school an' took on the mother work. I helped her more, an' aided Dad a tad less. I wished ta leave school, but Dad said no. In other things he was easy, but not that. Yet I learned much more a who I am from Dad than from school. I cut back ta four days a week.

"His smithing shop went well, an' the next year he took on a help. 'Twas Adam Josephs. Highly reputed, he came from the next county. His father was a preacher, an' he much a that bent. He was four years my senior: polite, though rare ta smile, an' not a big talker. Seemed a good worker with Dad. His being nice in appearance, an' more kindly than mean, Rosie took ta' 'im. They got along, an' soon their eyes lit up when they glanced each other's way. 'Twasn't so long till they married.

"That year I passed exams an' left school. I turned ta helping Dad more in the shop, whilst yet assisting Rosie too.

"It went well awhile, an' then a dreadfull sad day Dad an' me went ta the mill in town for flour. We left the horse an' wagon at the veterinary stable. The horse being in need a looking after. We walked ta take lunch, an' then fetched a sack a flour an' a halfsack. I was near his size an' strength then, being a nineteen years. We shouldered the sacks an' set out. I reached for the full sack, but he insisted, an' I got the halfsack.

"'Twas a spring Saturday, the town abustle. I felt good ta be so alive, walking with Dad, talking loud about this an' that. A night rain had left the street muddy an' the walkway wet.

"Two tykes came skipping playfull on the stone walk. Weaving their childish, nimble way through the older folk. I moved a step aside so's ta miss stepping on the kids, an' kept speaking ta Dad behind me. But he didn't answer. I looked o'er my shoulder, an' a few steps back he'd gone down in the street. In the jostle, under the weight a the heavy bag, he'd misstepped an' tumbled ta the muddy road 'fore a two horse wagon. Dad was under as I turned ta see. It came out the worst a sadness. An ugly flour an' mud mess. He was gone that quick."

But for the high chop's rattle, I surely could a heard more soft sobs 'n my own.

(30) The other half

"So then we were three, as Adam had moved in. Already a fourth was expected. Rosie was with child.

"Soon there were problems. He was, as his dad, most deep in religion. Held strong, hard belief in things I was half certain he was wrong on. The bible held his every answer. An' when caught up, he'd wear a mean silence. Growls'd come from his eyes. Y'd feel 'im chewing back words his church disliked.

So's Adam an' Eve were the first alone.
That would be right.

They had three sons, Cain, Able an' Seth.
You got it.
But the three had no children, so how'd things get going?
Oh, they had many children.
With wives from where? Adam an' Eve being first alone.
"His eyes'd growl loud through a mean silence.

"Then there was Noah an' his ark. A boat made extra huge an' strong enough ta, for forty days, hold two animals a every sort in the world an' their food. Animals who didn't go about fighting or eating each other. So what did they eat? Some only eat other animals.

"An' tell me about all the birds? The simplest dullard knows no bird can stay aloft forty days an' nights. So how'd old Noah go about catching two a each? An' who can tell apart males an' females? Did he never get two males? How'd that work out?"

Loud chuckles came in the darkness. We were bouncing good on the high chop, all hugging seats. Yet Gorden went on as 'twas the calmest day in his mind. His voice rarely broke.

"Then ya throw in the problem a the huge wild African elephant, the great white north bears, an' the fierce big tigers a the East! Did he go afar o'er the whole world finding 'em? Or did they get an invite an' swim all across the vast ocean ta 'im, along with the many other strange animals we all know roam through the world? The more ya think on it, the bigger silly bumfuggled {confused} mess it appears. An' the more clearly absurd the bloody story's foolishness grows.

"The Adam an' Eve question wasn't mine. Dad spoke on it once. He believed in God, yet not in the church, an' never went on about it. Insisted each must take their own path. He was most beautyfully not pushy on so many things. More oft waiting till asked, he'd offer a good thought modestly. It would be one a fine clarity, yet not delivered with bluster. Dad quietly knew he believed.

"Adam was the direct opposite. He loudly believed he knew. With Dad gone, he spoke out. In the shop he knew as well, though he hadn't mastered the smithing. Again his eyes'd growl when ya had ta show 'im the right way 'tmust be done.

"But four years my senior, he needed ta act a father ta me. 'Twas his sworn duty ta save my hell bound soul. Even disliked my longer hair, though he could find nothing against it in his bible. So there were problems. Recalling my father's ways, an' considering sweet Rosie's peace, I held back my words.

"I was growing so fond a Mary, at age one. Yet I saw Adam didn't want my influence on her. We spoke seldom of religion. He was giving up on my doubtfull soul. I deeply pondered leaving 'fore I'd become o'erly attached ta that beautyfull niece. Mary was not my child ta form, as I wasn't Adam's.

"His smithing improved, yet it could a grown farther with small enthusiasms. He'd not yet a mastered all the skills, yet he didn't discourage me from leaving as his teacher, so I did.

"Prospects were good. My hands were strong an', thanks ta Dad, they had fine smithing. Yet I traveled afar with no purpose, moping about, squandering my modest savings. I found a bigger, louder world out there than expected, yet it came on small an' dull without lovely Rosie an' giggling little Mary in it.

"I'd sunk ta the bottom a the keg in a London pub one afternoon, my fortune being a few coins in my pocket. 'Twas a poor place near the docks. Mostly for sailing crew. There, across the room, three scrawny ne'er-do-wells went about bothering a young loner like myself. So I stepped in ta help even things up. Taking measure a my smithing arms, the three backed out, throwing behind an insult at my long hair.

"Whilst we two victors sat an' spoke as long friends, the loner rewarded me with a bite an' ale, as I'd secretly hoped he might. Hearing me out regarding my poor situation, he strongly suggested I join 'im that night as crewman aboard the *Vengeferth*. They held an opening. Captain, he assured, was a good man who'd approve me. I'd never held a thought on turning pirate, yet he struck me as a good sort, an' any situation would save me at the moment. For one at such a low point, 'twas fate's best fortune ta fall inta such a fine ship an' crew," Gorden concluded with heavy sleep in his voice.

He'd lost a man ta snoring, Likely Dessinger. Gorden's tale well kept me awake. It felt nicely calming ta travel a time on a freedom escape ta dry land away from that vast ocean, even if 'twas in the mind. I snuggled in. Usual whale singing was under the chop. With it in my mind, Gorden's story eased me ta a more restfull sleep aboard our well lost smallboat.

(31) Singing, an' about a rummaging party

That night the chop smoothed. We got rest. Our sleeps were eased by our minds' escape in Gorden's story, an' the lowering chop. Our tied-down roof kept' the boat dark, helping us sleep late. Cheered, Reed struck up a song at morn mess, an' all joined in. Many tunes later, we'd crooned well past mess.

There was humor in the singing. Six weren't bad voices. Dessinger was best. Him singing *Battle a Benburb* was pure heaven, an' we'd oft beg it from 'im. We'd hum softly under. The humor was Heitman. He much enjoyed jumping on each word with endless, enthused hand clapping. His timing was fine, yet he hadn't one good ear ta tell 'im his voice forever strayed desperately off the tune. Early in the trip he stood on a seat foot stomping. Captain quick warned 'im our boat couldn't take it. Though his drone grew most tiresome, his joy in singing kept us from revealing ta 'im his vocal failings. Those still awake, oft sang songs softly as he snored. Called 'em Heitman's lullabies.

That noon I slouched o'er a keg in the endless torture a soaking my slow-healing palms. Reed sat taking his turn at the fishing, the carrot top blowing about. 'Twas growing toward Gorden's wavy look. He turned ta me, seeking answers. This, his first voyage being so abnormal an' briefly ended, he was keen ta hear a the normal pirating days he'd thus far missed. Using up some a our long tiresome time, an' taking my mind from my aching palms, I enjoyed savoring my answers ta Reed.

"So how does the *Vengeferth* divvy up her loot?" He asked.

I understood. He'd heard child's stories a exciting pirate riches, buried treasure chests an' such. As well, I saw a man's own payment is where his strongest interest lies. So I breathed deep an' straightened.

"I'll say how 'twas done aboard our *Vengeferth*. Yet, the vessel being lost, the future seems unlikely ta ever come 'round the same wonderfull way. Any pirate Captain's all his own man aboard ship. He does things his way.

"'Board the Vengeferth, 'twas joyous fun when we came a' port, heaved anchor, an' divvied the trinkets. 'Twas each man's birthday an' Christmas times five, maybe ten. Depended on the wealth of boats we took. No different from the fishing you're doing there. A' times we caught a big one, yet oft far from it, waifs struggling such that we felt the need ta give a handout.

"It began beautyfull sunny days when our rummaging party hoisted aboard chests with shiny trinkets an' cash loot. We'd all cheer an' sing loud as chests came o'er the rail, their heft far exaggerating. Rummagers were met as conquering heroes, though all knew 'twas far more the trinkets we wildly cheered."

"I bet ya layed eyes on some full chests a fine glitter," dreamy eyed Reed pondered, bouncing the bait on his line.

"Aye, I have a' times, yet not so oft.

"'Fore our shopping crew went aboard a ship ta rummage, we welcomed the ship's Captain aboard as our hostage guest. I was there many a time ta enjoy Captain Werthman's fine talk ta worried Captains. They'd been well searched for boot pistols, sleeve daggers an' such tomfoolery. I recall one brashly meant ta board with two weapons hid on his person.

He an' Captain had a fine chat:

"*Captain. Ya surprise me bringing aboard your weapons for unfriendly purpose. Appeared they weren't intended as gifts.*"

"'*Twas only for my own defense, sir.*"

"*Against forty? A pityfull defense. Ya take me a fool.*"

"*By acting a grievous offense, you begin our barter at a poor place. Two hid weapons cost ya two fingers a my choosing. Foolish words have grown your debt a finger. Any you choose.*"

"That Captain's eyes widened an' his shoulders sank. His hands crossed in front, as though one could protect the other. The front hand shook, whilst rubbing the other's back.

"But sir I, I, I--" he sputtered.

"Do ya play the piano, sir?" Captain Werthman plied.

"Ah, oh, ah, no, not at all."

"It'll be hard learning. I mean should ya decide ta do so."

"But, but, sir, 'tis barbaric. I've surrendered. The ship's yours."

"Aye, ya surrendered with guns up your sleeve, then insulted my good sense ta my face. What punishment would ya mete out ta me an' my men should we set foot aboard your vessel, each with two weapons? Would ya be so barbaric as ta kill us all?"

"But, but, but not if ya surrendered?"

"Be most carefull, sir. Ya already bartered away three fingers, an' those words just put a fourth in doubt."

"But, but," he sputtered. "So what's it ya ask? I lost! Ya won!"

"We've wasted enough time. I'll explain quick. Oft I give a friendly Captain a pick a the trinkets rummaged from his ship. It would be in return for his help pointing out where the booty's hid. He might select a pricey item. A' times he'll choose a sentimental one. Should he beg a low value item with sentiment, I oft gift a second item a my choosing. Yet when a Captain's forgets ta mention sizable trinkets found stowed on his ship, he'll reboard his ship minus fingers. Do ya see where I'm going here?"

"I, I, but... Yes 'tis quite clear."

"Fine. Write out the whereabouts a cash an' trinkets aboard your vessel. Y'll choose back no item from the trinkets we find. Yet ya may earn back fingers now owed, thus making it so easy for ya ta someday play the piano quite nicely."

(32) Half shark caught, an' Reed warned

"'Tis how we went about finding cash an' trinkets. People are most fond a their fingers. Attached ta 'em ya might say. Those who chose back an item were so happy, as they found it far distant from their expectation. Some Captains chose costly items, clearly planning ta keep 'em, though they hadn't been their own. All hearts own an ounce a larceny," I grinned, pulling up my sore, pruney hands from the sweetwater.

"What about divvying up that grand loot? How's that done?"

Reed asked, youthfully eager. Not noticing a pull on his line.

"Tend ta the fish on your line. I'll dry these prunewrinkled, aching hands so's Doc can rewrap 'em. Then we'll enjoy away more a the day explaining that sweet answer.

Gorden scrambled ta help Reed with the smaller shark on his line. 'Twas truly smaller when hauled o'er the side. A bigger beast chomped her in two but two foot out, thus ending the tussle. Didn't leave so much for our bellies, yet saved us the trouble a killing 'im whilst avoiding loss a fingers.

A close view a the larger brute's chomping teeth an' saucer eyes jolted Reed an' widened his own eyes near the size a the shark's. Most smiled but none laughed. We'd been there a time.

Captain Werthman didn't smile. Likely he was seeing the white deliver Jonesy's body inta his lap. No humor there.

Doc dried my pained palms, put fish oil on, an' rewrapped 'em. I sidled back by Reed. He was disheveled. Appeared he could use my story ta clear the shark's fearfull fright from his mind. So I started back in as though nothing went by.

"First off, there ya went again saying it as though 'tis in the future. Our *Vengeferth's* on the ocean floor. Slim's the chance Captain might e'er take another ship out. I expect ta keep my own feet on dry land when I reput 'em there. 'Twas meant as my last voyage. I'm more ta that bent now. This trip's got us all bumfuggled. I doubt I'm the only man who'll bid the seafaring life fare-the-well after this most wearisome trip"

'Twas low chop an' quiet. All ears caught my words, though I spoke as ta only Reed. None, including our Captain, spoke out ta disagree with my speculation there.

"Now, I'll tell a the wonderfull paydays aboard the *Vengeferth* which you came aboard too late ta see. But I must remind ya. Should ya sign on with another ship, 'twill likely differ. It comes from the Captain. He makes the rule. If he wants ta keep the crew happy, an' knows how, like our fair Werthman, 'tis better than fine. But 'tis not oft the way. There are fierce Captains a' sea, feared by their crew as much as their foes. Oft many a their crewmen are kidnapped slaves. Consider the boat ya sign on. Take good measure a any Captain sign on with."

I had back Reed's attention. In his easy youthfullness, our carrot top'd quickly put behind 'im the sharks fierce scare.

"We enjoyed magical paydays aboard the *Vengeferth*. When a rummaging gang returned from a richer ship an' hoisted the glittering booty o'er the side, me an' Captain first spread it about the deck. Men gleefully inspected, strolling about, minds dancing amongst the gold an' jewels asparkle in the sun. Each was weighing which trinkets he'd choose on payday.

"Were he deserving, the hostage Captain chose back a trinket 'fore he left. Were he foolish, a' times we lopped fingers.

"All swag entered our Captain's locker ta safe keep. Nothing was divvied whilst a' sea. Trinkets or money in a crew's hands begs gambling, an' thievery whilst men sleep. Losing gamblers too oft call winners cheats an' fights can cause grave injury.

Payday came when we were anchored an ready ta go ashore. We spent a day cleaning ship, 'fore payday. 'Twas clearly the Captain's scheme ta get the ship whistle clean for next trip. We humored 'im. Just laughed like good school children, an' went on whistling away a day shining up our fine ship, whilst dreaming of shiny trinkets we'd seen an' planned ta soon pocket."

(33) About divvying the loot.

'Twas unsurprising that young Reed was fancifully caught up in my clear recollections. Yet the others listened, an' seemed charmed as well. As though they'd not been there themselves. Like we all could escape our miserable situation ta go back an' live it all out one more magical time.

"Don't be so mindless as ta imagine every ship we took was filthy rich with cash an' jewels," I went on. "Most weren't. Many had few trinkets an' monies ta feed our Captain's locker. We took amounts a cargo a' times. *Vengeferth* was small ta carry many goods. We oft took ten, twelve ships or more, 'fore Captain stood up after stowing a heist an' bawled *'Tis time for a payday*. His words were greeted by wild cheering, an' singing. A sip a rum might be portioned, an' the men'd party all eve.

"Next morn we'd be swift sailing for a near port. We'd drop anchor an' whistle away a day cleaning ship. So many men got ta whistling, those came ta be known as whistle days.

"Then payday came. Captain, Doc, an' me awoke ta an early meal. We then hauled our cache from the Captain's room ta beautyfully festoon the deck with trinkets, whilst the crew below ate Cookie's best morn mess. Sunrise set that deck asparkle so wondrously, as though 'twas afire. Crew oohed, aahed, an' giggled, climbing on deck ta sit in a circle about our sparkling fire. 'Twas spread there for all ta see that every piece they'd seen stowed in the Captain's locker was accounted for.

"Finally Captain went out an' chose a trinket. All cheered. I, amid cheers, then chose a trinket. Soon after, Doc, an' Cookie went. Then followed each crewman in order according ta their time aboard ship. Captain again went out for a trinket an' we all went again in turn. It continued till the deck was empty an' our pockets full. All in queue who failed ta get a trinket last time around, were counted out a fair cash sum.

"'Twas time ta divvy cash money. A modest sum went ta supply our ship. Captain, Doc, Cookie, an' me got a small bonus. The rest was divided even amongst us all. An' there ya had it.

"All could then jump in a smallboat an' head ashore, but 'twas the rare man who didn't wait a time there on deck. We stood in queue awaiting a turn at the table where Captain an' Doc sat an' discussed the worth a each trinket held by a crewman. They gave opinions on the value crewmen should expect ta receive from a pawnbroker or charlatan aport. 'Twas ta keep the men from being fiddled. Captain'd say: *Tis worth forty-five pounds at least. Ask fifty-five, an' if they won't offer even forty-two, I'll give ya forty-two. Or, if they go low on ya, just tell 'em the Captain'll give forty-two, an' likely they'll match it.*

"Don't expect such help from another Captain ya serve. Ships might have a helping purser, yet don't o'er trust 'im."

Reed hung on each word, nodding. So much jawing, though well enjoyed, wore on me. I excused myself an' moved ta my spot in the bow ta snuggle in an' nap till mess.

Enough story for the day, we agreed at mess ta leave the captain's eve story till the next night.

Chop was low that starry night, an' the continuous mournfull singing a the whales was near scary in its loudness. I lay awake hours, not pondering huge whales, as I might have. 'Twas the state a our circumstances that nagged my mind. Our food situation was poor an' growing poorer. We'd opened some food kegs ta find but stinking rottage. Sadly, the second keg a salt pork we'd saved, an' looked fondly on, went spoiled. Kegs should store in a cool hold, not sit warm in the sun. I'm sure opening 'em twice as we started, hastened their ruin as well.

Nor did it rain as oft as we wished. Yet we were always good for water, as we'd fill many kegs when it came. Our sail's runoff filled 'em well. A diet a raw fish alone, so tiresome, seemed bound ta happen soon. Yet some meat was on the way.

(34 The mosquito an' tortoise

I awoke late an' tired. Others'd finished morn mess. No man was purposely wakened, lest he was thrashing about. Sleep was time most oft spent in a dream world more pleasant than the one we woke to. 'Twas escape from our situation's boredom.

I finished mess, an' here came Doc the torturer, looking ta soak my bloody aching hands. There was no way ta be smaller an' harder ta find. Thankfully the following night the ache in my hands finally quieted, an' in the next days 'twent from less ta gone. Doc's fresh water soaks an' fish oil did the trick. Yet, at the time, had I a third, nonpainfull hand, I might a swatted 'im away like a pest mosquito.

Ta mention mosquitos, one bite me near noon. I thought little on it. Mashed the bloodsucker inta red smear with the back a my right wrist. My palms were pained by the act. We'd carried our share a the bothersome buggers aboard the *Vengeferth*. Couldn't rid ourselves a 'em till they all went down with the ship. 'Twas a most pittyfull way ta rid ourselves of 'em. Yet we tried ta be mindfull a the least blessing.

A long hour after the critter bit, that itch on my arm finally reached my slow-thinking brain ta ask: *From whence in this wide world might a tiny bug come ta find our boat after forty-some days adrift?* I slapped myself upside the head, again stupidly paining my palm. My bleary old eyes widened.

"*Captain!*" I cried out, as though he sat in the next shire, not across from me. "**I was bit by a mosquito! Here on my arm! We must be nearing some mosquito infested land!**"

I showed my bumped up mosquito bite like 'twas a prized possession ta brag on. For the moment 'twas. The men eyed the bite an' grew excited. They went ta swiveling their heads, squinting their eyes, an' scouring the distance for the bug's home. 'Twas ta no avail, yet hopes were up.

"Don't get your excitement so high, men," Doc warned. "I've read the buggers get caught in a squall an' carried hundreds a miles a' sea. Even a' times across this ocean."

"Seems sadly possible," I sighed. "Yet mayhap less likely."

The men nodded, an' mumbled agreement, craving hope.

"Perhaps the bloody bug blew o'er from a near ship," Dessinger offered. "Our *Vengeferth* had more 'n a few."

Again the men nodded hopefully.

I jested, "Sure hope who lost 'im comes looking for 'im."

Captain Werthman guffawed a half second ahead a the rest, an' all had a good, long laugh. Some ta tears.

Catching his breath, Captain offered, "Wil Devoe, ya must pen a tome about this trip, as charged. I swear if ya don't, I'll not have ya aboard my next ship," he clearly jested, as he well heard me say I planned ta stay ashore when we found land.

"I take ya as a man a your word, Captain," I answered lively. "'Tis music ta my tired ears. In fact the far best promise I've heard all day. Even all year, an' perhaps my entire life."

"Aye, but 'twas quite in jest," Captain came back. "'Fore the ink's dry, I'll turn it around. If ya *fail* ta write the book, I'll take ya a' sea an' have ya work the riggin. 'Tis my final word."

"Aye, then rest assured the tome'll be writ," I groused.

Captain's easy praise was pleasant, whilst it showed his deep confidence on us ending this tiresome odyssey safely a' land.

That moment, Gorden, who searched the horizon, cried he'd seen something. Thinking a the mosquito's home we'd been jawing on, we were disappointed ta follow his gaze. Something floated a distance out. Gorden's sharpest eyes soon made it out ta be a tortoise at nap, warming in the sun. We espied 'em oft aboard the *Vengeferth*. Saw 'em as good luck fellow friends. This one had the bad luck ta be seen as much needed foodstuff.

Oars ta the powlocks, we eased toward our unsuspecting prey. Reed climbed out on the portside mast as we sidled up by her. He managed ta tie a rope on a leg an' kill her quick with our dagger. 'Twas a sad way ta treat a peacefull fellow traveler, yet all our stomachs agreed 'twas survival's need.

Pulling her aboard was a heavy chore. Sharks smell blood an' come nosing around. Modest in size, she managed ta come aboard 'fore the sharks showed. 'Twas done quick.

Fortunately the chop was low, an' sky cloudless the next two days. The hot sun dried strips a tortoise meat set atop kegs, an' nary a morsel bounced off. We so enjoyed food unfishflavored. 'Twas a mean chew, yet after many day a soft fishy meat, the chewing work was appreciated nearly as much as the meat's unfishy taste. We ate it sparingly, saving much. The dried meat left o'er, filled a small keg an' would surely store a time.

(35) Whales sing an' jump

That night whale songs, which forever lulled us asleep, were so mournfully loud as ta keep me awake the longest. The restless giants felt most near. Were rain felt, I swear I'd a took it for spout water. Might one sidle up an' raise a big espying eye o'er the rail ta satisfy some curiosity? *Oh, that's the appearance a the happy pig chorus. Or, that's the bloke dreaming a the loudest pig.* Yet maybe, *that's the rude one whose ugly snorts step on my beautyfull song.* I rolled up a cover coat under my head ta pillow the noise. It left me cooler, but I then found sleep.

As we ate early mess, the monsters took ta breaching. Four of 'em giving us a show, frolicking like happy tykes showing themselves off. Trying ta outjump each other in turn. Not so close we felt the spray, yet nearer than we needed, feeling precarious in our smallboat. Their splashup well rocked us.

"What do ya s'ppose they sing about?" Reed groused. Clearly we'd all lost sleep ta their singing the last night.

"Could be snoring the night away," I offered. "Though now they're clearly bragging on who jumped higher an' splashed bigger. Yet their sounds do always vary, as if they're jawing back an' forth. Just gabbing away I s'ppose. 'Tis thought one can hear another half an ocean away, an' I wouldn't bet against it."

"But they go on forever. What might there be in their dark world ta jaw so on about?" Reed pondered, shaking his head.

"Well, I hear they live ta a ripe age," I smiled. "Likely they're complaining a their many ailments. 'Tis what old folks do."

Captain burst inta hearty guffaws, as did the others.

"My long held idea," Doc offered, finding his breath, "is that the playfull jumps amount ta barnacle parties. It's how they rid themselves of nuisances that cling to 'em, same as a ship's hull. Clearly they have great fun with it, so they sing songs."

"Surely 'tis fine backscratching," Captain put in. "They're a cheerfull lot, singing an' showing themselves off as well."

We watched a time, till they ended their sporting about.

Then Doc got me soaking my palms. Doc needed more patients. With but one patient ta bother, he had much time on his hands ta fuss with my hands which were doing fine. He was always looking at 'em an' checking on 'em. Wouldn't leave 'em alone. Doc couldn't keep his hands ta 'imself, nor could I.

Slumped o'er the soaking keg, eyes closed, enjoying the cool breeze, I felt Reed sidle up. He came asking me ta fill 'im in on the *Vengeferth's* barnacle parties. 'Twas another best part a the pirate life he'd heard much jawed of, yet missed out on. His question was a welcome invitation ta get me going, enjoying another escape sailing on memory's breeze away from the growing uncertainty in our tiresome situation.

(36) About barnacle parties

"Course ya know, Mister Reed, pirates might need ta call out their ship's top speed for survival any time," I started in, after straightening myself a bit, coughing, an' breathing deep. "We must be ready ta use every smidgeon a speed our ship can muster. Running for our lives, we must truly fly like the wind. Mostly 'tis needed ta steer clear a well-armed military boats with heavy guns. They seem ta firmly believe 'tis their business ta bother us, so they go against us every chance they get.

"What robs a ship a the least ounce a speed, if we allow, is barnacles clinging ta the hull. Add on the seaweed they collect as we roll, an' the mess drags on us. Barnacle scraping's a most unfavored chore, yet a smooth hull means our life. If we get lazy on cleaning our hull, we're cannon fodder.

"There's more good sense ta keeping the hull clean than holding a ship's speed up. Barnacles grow as they cling along," I went on. "They get chomping deeper in, digging worm holes, weakening the wood. Keeping the hull clean, we keep her strong. No worm holes.

"'Twas oft different aboard the ships that brought us our money an' trinkets. Greedy owners kept 'em moving, making profits. Down time costs money, as does a shipyard cleaning bill. Crews oft ride worm-hole-weak coffins just waiting on a strong storm ta tear their hull asunder. Money grubbing owners don't set foot aboard 'em. That land lubber's life's not on the line. He'll invest in insurance, an' keep 'em running till suddenly they sink. Surprise! No wondering why."

"Many ships pump water out day an' night. Young crewmen miss how bad 'tis. Don't hear what a boat's telling 'em," I explained, stretching my aching back. Reed nodded along.

"Military are different. They've men with time on their hands. Little ta do but scrape a hull. They oft sit leeching off taxpaying folk. Fortunately they feel a need ta carry aboard many heavy cannons that slow 'em. Yet when three or four ships with sly Captains hang together, we need high speed an' maybe an ounce a luck ta get through. Our magic guns gave us the advantage, even against military. But we avoided 'em. Sinking 'em gained us naught but a high price tag on our head.

"Back ta barnacle parties. We'd find a cove a mile or two from a nice little port. Captain cozied us in close ta shore, an' we lightened ship, offloading guns an' kegs ta smallboats an' up the beach. 'Tis work, yet only a start," I assured Reed, pulling my pruney hands from the keg an' stretching my stiff back.

"Guns on the beach," I soon went on, "we circled 'round a deepanchored post, aiming outward. 'Tis a defensive habit seldom usefull. Yet a foe coming from any direction, *might* eat a cannonball if we hurry. A gun's moved back against the post ta shoot. Post takes the kickback. 'Tis not an ideal arrangement, yet might do if necessary. Takes some men a while ta lug a gun ta the post through the sand. If the sand's soft ya mostly carry the monster. The setup appears fierce anyway."

"What if a man in a desperate hurry fired one with nothing ta take the kickback?" Reed asked, an interesting speculation.

"Don't know," I confessed. "No bloke tried it, so far as I know. Yet a drunken partier musta done it a time. If the kickback didn't put an end ta the dimwit, his Captain surely did.

"Gun'd likely land atop the post or another gun an' smash both ta smiodereens. Goodbye ta the crewman she alit on. He's *bound* ta wake up dead.

"Yet 'twould be an event ta see," I chuckled. "More so, seen well drunk. Kinda like Chinese sky sparklers.

"But anyhow, back ta the path," I laughed. *'Twas fun off the path*. "The boat lightened, at high tide we'd pull her ashore an' scrap the hull. Sweaty work, yet the easy part. Tip her one way, clean a side, roll her o'er an' do the other. Then set her aright so's we could sleep aboard. Many busy hands eased the work.

(37) The party part

"Whilst we crew scraped rubbish from the hull, Captain an' Doc'd row ta the near port for party stuff. They spruced up, trying their best ta appear unpiratelike. Got themselves looking pretty fine in attire we'd rummaged from ships. Hard ta recognize. They'd climb aboard a smallboat an' row out in their oft misfitted clothes an' far differing heights. Doc a full foot the shorter. Cyrano an' Copernicus they were, out ta find the world. We had ta chuckle viewing their backs."

Oops, how'd I forget they themselves listened? Captain caught the guilty thought writ on my face an' his laughter quick grew threefold. Twixt gales a mirth he soon gasped, "Aye ya forgot we each sit with two ears."

Doc was amused yet more—his hands slapping knees, face red, an' tears rolling down both cheeks.

"After the work we partied," I soon plunged on. "A reward for sweaty toil. Much a the party stuff we'd rummaged. Captain hoarded it away. Yet he'd find a new surprise in town. He also shopped a few supplies ta be laded aboard when we'd stop by after the party. Mayhap shop 'im a new wide-brim, were one ta be found.

"Doc 'd roust about hunting science books an' repair tools he didn't already own. We swore Doc's library an' tool bin might grow ta someday sink the ship. Kicking about, Doc'd get newspapers for the men, an' a novel or two for me as well. The important prize they mustn't fail ta haul back was a pig ready ta roast o'er a fire on the beach--one hefty, or two smaller ones.

"Captain an' Doc'd be back, pig smellin fine on the fire, an' dusk coming on when the hull was clean an' the ship aright.

"One way or other, most oft by volunteer, two men were chose ta stay sober, same as Captain an' Doc. The four earned some bonus cash ta party sober. 'Twas security meant ta save us from intruders, an' from our own drunken foolishness.

"So the party was on. We drank rum, swam, played runabout games, ate meat, drank rum, sang, told stories, drank rum, ate meat, played games, slept a spell, an' went back at it.

"Three days the party boomed on. Then we ran out a breath. Farthest from my prime, I went in early eves, yet was amongst the first ta fold. Few partied the third eve. 'Twas a rest time.

"Hardest job came at high tide, setting the ship afloat. Pulling her ashore felt near fun. Pushing her out was farthest from fun. Though lightened, *Vengeferth* was no feather. Maybe pushing was really so much harder than pulling, or maybe 'twas the rum we'd swilled. Ya couldn't wade ta deep water an' pull her. Must push. Success could seem doubtfull, yet, in the end, we always managed the task. Took a pityfull while a' times.

"Then another chore, our final mean one, lading guns an' cargo back aboard. Lading guns aboard was more certainly possible than pushing the ship off the beach, yet as tiresome. The heavy guns were slogged through the sand ta smallboats, then out ta the ship, an' winched aboard. Ya had ta go so slow. Broken toes mashed fingers, an' worse, could carelessly be had. With the guns aboard, lading other cargo back was easy as a biscuit. All were dog tired, yet the end was in sight.

"That was it. We'd stop a' port, collect Captain's ordered goods, an' head out riding easy on a clean hull," I concluded, suggesting, "I'm hungry. Let's enjoy mess." The word *enjoy* I meant as humor. It flew past their tired minds.

O'er mess we agreed we'd had enough storytelling for a day. But Captain Werthman promised ta finally tell us straight out the next eve the story on how he came by the magical guns.

Gritty fog began ta creep in that eve as we tied the tarp o'er. 'Twas the heaviest mist ta find us since we came aboard the smallboat. Oddly there was still some small chop. Ya expect fog ta wrap ya in only on dead still nights.

(38) In the fog

Next morn this oldster was first ta receive nature's call, as usual. Chop was down ta dead smooth. My head popped up ta find us closed within a small, hazy world. The wide expanse we gazed on was shrunk down ta a bedding closet. 'Twas a heavy, damp space so full a thick silence ya didn't wish ta blink an eye, for fear it'd be heard. My heart thump seemed loud though 'twas far less than excited.

Damp mist crawling about isn't new ta any seaman. Yet I've never enjoyed its dank smell. Thick fog has for me the feel a dream whispers wanting ta turn nightscares.

My business done quick, I ducked back under for more sleep, but it didn't come. I expected ta soon hear another soul astir. Nor did that occur. Strangely, neither did a single man snort aloud. The usual was a happy pig chorus. Seemed each man'd fallen attune with the heavy fog an' joined its thick silence, even Heitman whose ear never got it right.

Finally, I went up ta watch the mist burn off. Felt early, yet 'twas uncertain. The sun might be some off the horizon. Only a small blue sky hole showed straight above. Bit by slowly bit, the hole sucked back in each direction. The same empty view we'd gazed on forever promised ta show itself in all its boredom. Fog burning down was something I didn't watch. Felt nearly as unexciting as watching grass grow. Yet that morn 'twas only so whilst the blue patch widened some, an' then widened more. Then very slowly a half vague, ghostly crow's nest began poking up from the mist dead ahead. It appeared but a stone's throw away, maybe two, yet less than half real.

I heard a noise. A glance espied Captain's head stick up.

"Morn Wil, I--"

I cut 'im off sharp, pointing, "Am I seeing that, Captain?" My hoarse whisper begged. "Pray tell me 'tis no dream."

His gaze followed my straight finger, an' he spoke naught.

"Tell me 'tis no dream, Captain," I lowly beseeched, eyes glued ta the crow's nest still so vague.

"No dream, Wil. None a' tall. 'Tis the rescue ship we despair for. She's there in the fog. Close enough ta near touch."

We quick called the men out, an' all gazed in breathless silence, mouths agape. Mists artfully melted away, displaying masts, then a ship more beautyfull ta our eyes than any comely temptress one might 'imagine. Coyly, she unveiled herself in the vapors, like a butterfly easing from her cocoon. Men knelt. There were small sobs that our ordeal was done, an' no dry eye.

Soon Gorden's sharp gaze read from her bow, *Crazy Cousin*, an' we fell out laughing. Who should come ta our rescue but our *Crazy Cousin*? All layed claim ta crazy cousins, yet none half so beautyfull. Finally Doc suggested getting oars ta the powlocks, an' we jumped on it. Reed an' Gorden were rowing hard 'fore the rest a us had our boat's cover full off.

As we neared, the *Crazy Cousin* sat silent, suggesting abandonment. No breathing soul stood on deck, though the sun showed itself well up. Mainsail was the only canvas. It hung in a useless manner, aloose at the bottom. Should a breeze come on, she'd clearly flutter like a banner, not fill out as a sail.

We slowed ta a drift, scratching our heads. What might be found aboard? Dead bodies, dying folks, old skeletal bones, or nobody a' tall? Might we be greeted by a plague that wiped out the crew? Also in question was how we were ta board. We'd no grappling hook ta toss up, catch the rail, an' give us means.

She was a mid-sized freighter with few portals, yet there were some. Clearly we must climb up an' break through one.

"I'll go in first," Doc offered low. "If there's disease, I might diagnose it and know what we're dealing with."

"A fine plan, Doc," Captain also spoke low. "But I measure we'll need three men on shoulders ta reach the portal. Reed, our lightest, takes the meat hammer up an' breaks in. When he drops a ratline, you're next man up ta consider the situation."

Why were we speaking in low tones? It wasn't so clear. Mayhap we spoke low being the air was funeral hushed. Might there be dead folks about we had no wish ta waken? "Let's sidle up an' thump her," I muttered, low. "Might get an answer."

As we came on, I saw her hull 'neath the waterline was thick with seaweed. Legions a barnacles must cling under, chomping deep wormholes in this *Crazy Cousin's* hull. Such neglect suggested she'd be little longer afloat.

As Captain reared back ta thump her, a big, heavenly chorus sang aloud. He held the oar back, froze. We gazed about. Did heaven's angels sing out: *don't do that*? The music continued on as a vaguely familiar religious tune with muffled words.

"Must be interrupting Sunday morn service, men," Captain quick gleaned an' smiled. "'Tis clearly our prayer's answer."

(III) Aboard *the Crazy Cousin*

(39) We board

"Best bang her high up," I warned. "Hull appears shaky."

"Noticed," Captain answered, an' boomed her high as he could reach. He'd swung the oar wide, an' the three booms were loud. A face soon showed o'er the rail above us.

"That's enough banging," a young man's voice called down cheerily, yet not so loud. "We've heard it. You replacements are bothering a funeral. Reverend Jo sent me up to let you in. You're rather late, but we're quite pleased you found us."

"He'll *let us in*. Spoke like the purest land lubber," Captain whispered low. Then he called up, "The best way ya can let us in is ta drop a line for us ta climb up."

"I see. Of course. It'll take a moment. My brother'll help. It's heavy line," he called, an' left 'fore Captain could say 'tis but a one man task ta secure line ta the mast an' feed it o'er the rail.

Quickly the lad was back calling low, "Here it comes." as a heavy line crashed down on the mast lashed ta our port side, thus bouncing the boat severely an' knocking us all off our feet. Thankfully, no one fell outside the boat.

"Sorry. We didn't quite intend that. Are you all well?"

"Aye, we're quite fine," Captain assured, as we scrambled ta restand. "But 'tis best if ya secure one end a the line around the mast, then feed down the other end for us ta climb up."

"Oh yes. Good idea. I don't suppose you can toss an end a that one up. No. We'll get a second line."

Whilst the young blokes went for another line, we pulled aboard the line they'd nearly injured us with. None whispered on what dunderheads we'd found, for fear words might carry. They were, after all, young lads trying their best ta help us aboard. I'm sure all the crew was, like me, wondering what they meant calling us the replacements.

Soon they were back lowering a line, with one calling out,

"We wrapped it three times around the mast this time."

Reed tugged on it, an' the line felt good. But he got six foot up an' she came aloose. Reed an' the line splashed inta the water near the boat. He jumped from the water quick, glad he'd neither knocked his head nor met a shark hanging about.

"Ya didn't tie a knot in her, did ya?" Captain called up.

"No. It would have been a fine idea though," he called back.

"No worry," our so patient Captain answered. "The third try's bound ta be a lucky charm."

"Likely it would, but that was the last rope," he informed.

"Nonsense. Fetch one a the crew ta go up an' bring a line down from the riggin. I see one from here."

"The Captain's the only man aboard who can climb up there, and he's kind of old. He's also down sick in bed."

"Where's the rest a the crew?"

"The old crew left out a while back. Another crew's being sent out to drive the ship. Are you not them?"

"No. Our boat sank an' we're lost a' sea," Captain Werthman told, then asked, "So none aboard can climb the riggin?"

"Some of us tried going up there, as we'd seen the crewmen so easily do. One man was catching on. He was doing pretty well, but that's his funeral music you hear."

"Sorry ta hear that. We'll send a man in through a portal then, if 'tis good with ya," Captain Werthman called. "Can ya open one for us?"

"There's a portal open on the other side where we pump the extra water out. You might use that one."

"That sounds good. How oft do ya pump out extra water?"

"Two folks work the pump always. We take turns. An' one thing more. Reverend Jo said to ask if you men are Christians."

The Captain glanced about at us.

"Ya hear that music, don't ya," I hinted low.

"Aye," he assured, then called up as we began rowing our way around the ship, "aye, we hold a Christian bent down here. Tell me, how many folks are aboard this vessel?"

"Only forty three souls aboard now, due to this funeral."

We pondered the information so cheerfully delivered. 'Twas most distressing an' depressing. Our rescue ship appeared in the midst a disaster, likely progressing near the end. Most aptly named, the *Crazy Cousin* seemed in need a rescue worse 'n ourselves. 'Twas written in gray on all our faces. We traded questioning glances, slowly shaking heads. Some slumped, hands holding brows above teary eyes.

"At least it seems no plague's aboard," Doc sighed.

Reed, our slightest man, couldn't climb the riggin ta fetch a line, so Captain sent up our next leanest, Dessinger. In short order he squeezed through the portal past much *extra* water gushing in spurts from a hose. He retrieved a line, an' we seven soon climbed aboard. The deck creaked 'neath my first step. That creak crawled up my leg an' went a cold shiver up my spine. Surely the others shivered as well. We'd securely tied on our escape boat. I say escape boat, as the smallboat we came on suggested greater seaworthiness than this ship. We felt likely ta need it ta escape this foundering *Crazy Cousin*.

(40) Reverend Jo sweeps in

Oliver an' Edward were the two nice landlubbing dimwits who'd so poorly tried ta help us board. They introduced themselves with a handshake ta each man as he climbed o'er the rail. Tall, thin, an' ramrod straight, they were brothers a few years older 'n I'd taken 'em ta be. Edward was sixteen years, an' Oliver eighteen. For folks so in dire circumstances, they were bright eyed an' cheerfull. Oliver did all the talking, whilst Edward did only the nodding but ta tell his name shaking each hand.

"Reverend Jo instructs you're to go to the dining room. He'll be along after service," Oliver told, leading with a light step.

The insides a freighting ships tell their age. They're never repaintedup. Everything aboard the *Crazy Cousin* said old an' dingy. No detail cheered us. In the small mess room, the brothers excused themselves an' returned ta the funeral. We sat at tired wooden tables with countless names carved in. Nobody spoke. We had so many questions.

Finally Captain advised, "I'll speak with this preacher Jo when he comes in, men. Try not ta wear badly desperate faces. Needn't force a smile, but try not ta show anger or unfriendliness, no matter what's said. We're guests. Don't rile 'im. He'll likely talk more if we're friendly. Worse that can happen is we ride our smallboat on our way. But for bashed hopes, we'll be none the worse than when we woke this morn."

"Captain Werthman, how could we think of leaving folks out here ta sink?" Doc accused.

"I've seen no smallboats, an' she's taking on *extra* water. If we can't save 'em, we needn't go down with 'em. 'Twould help them none. If ya see a drowning man an' ya can't swim, makes no sense ta jump in ta drown with 'im. We'll have ta see."

Reverend Jo swept in filling the room. I say swept, 'cause his brown swishing shepherd's robe brushed the deck as he strode briskly, suggesting a broom, as did his wide spread black beard. One hand held a bible, the other a tall shepherd's crook.

We assumed his ta be funeral attire. But no, 'twas his usual dress as his flock's shepherd. Be assured a shepherd's crook is useless an' unwieldy aboard ship. Nor is a long robe the best.

He came in with the same cheeriness a voice as his two simple, young agents, "Hello gentlemen--"

The two spoken words startled Gorden ta his feet interrupting, "Adam Josephs! 'Tis *you* behind that big beard!"

"Jamie is it you?" Revered Jo recognized, an' they stepped up hugging like the best a old friends.

Having heard Gorden's story, all knew a Adam. We sat amazed ta find his sister's smithing husband as a preacher out on this ocean. How the devil'd a smithing brother-in-law get out here leading a flock on this foundering *Crazy Cousin*?

They jumped ta babbling questions, neither stopping ta give answer, "How are ya? How'd ya get here? How's the family?"

Till the Captain barked, "Whoa up! 'Fore ya jaw on about family an' all, lets discuss the desperation a your sinking ship."

"Oh we have no desperation," Jo assured cheerily. "We're not sinking, just waiting on the new crew. That's who we thought you were when you knock the hull. The boys say you're not them though. But as good Christians you're welcome to stay safe here. The new crew'll be along soon."

"So what happened ta the old crew?" Captain asked, eyes closed, his thumb an' forefinger pinching the bridge a his large nose, as I'd seen 'im appear oft times at the chess board.

"We sent them back ta send out a new one. That crew wasn't acceptable. We couldn't stop them from using such terrible language in front of the women and children, and looking at the women as well. We sent them home with money to hire a new crew and send it. The new crew should show any day."

"I see. Your boys say you're pumping *extra* water from the ship. How much *extra* water is there?" Captain asked, holding his voice calm, as though 'twasn't the scariest a questions.

"I don't know. I haven't checked. It's only down in the basement. We stay the next level up, so it's no bother. Our men keep the pump going, as the Captain insisted, so I doubt there's much left now. All the water should be out soon. Captain Smyth avowed we must pump till all the water's out. Seems, should we stop a short time, the pump won't restart."

"How deep was this *extra* water last time ya checked?"

"Captain Smyth kept measure of that. You can ask him, but I doubt he's of a right mind to give a clear answer."

"An' y've but one pump?" Captain glanced ta the heavens.

"We have two pumps on there on the second floor, but one broke shortly before the crew left. I thought I had them cured of their bad language, but when the pump broke they went back to it even worse. I warned that if they didn't clean up their language they'd have to leave. They didn't seem to mind the idea, so we sent them back to hire and send out another crew, being sure to include a man able to repair a broken pump."

"Smyth stayed aboard?" Captain asked, surprise in his voice.

"He was of a mind to go as well, but I saw he was clearly too ill. His condition has improved little since. Not so much of the body, but of the mind. I'm afraid he's over the edge."

"I see. We've the idea. Our ship sunk, an' we *might* be able ta repair this vessel enough ta return us all ta London."

"Oh no, we're bound for the colonies where a goodly number of heathen Indians are much in need of our strong religion. You're welcome to join us. But I wonder whether we should leave this spot. If the new crew arrived and was unable to find us, that would be bad for them."

"Don't worry Reverend Jo," Captain replied most seriously. "we'll write out a note an' leave it in a bottle."

Which caused some men small coughs ta hide laughter.

"That's an excellent idea, sir. I didn't get your name."

"Werthman. Captain Werthman, sir."

"Captain! You were a ship's Captain?"

"'Tis sadly the first time I've heard it put that way, but yes, I *was* a Captain, an' this my crew. We lost our ship in a squall."

"Oh. I'm unsure if I should turn this ship over to a crew who can't weather a storm. Seems it would be best to wait on the new crew. They're a bit late, but certain ta arrive soon."

"Ponder it," Captain urged, "whilst we look about an' see if we can help this *Crazy Cousin*. If one a your boys'll show Doc ta the sick Captain Smyth, the rest a us'll find our way around the ship. Ya just go on jawing with Gorden where I cut in.

"Dessinger, have one a the boys show ya around ta gauge the food an' fresh water supply. Heitman find out how much *extra* water she's carrying. Y'll need no guide ta find that. I'll be with Reed down by the broke pump. Report ta me there. DeVoe, step out ta the hallway with me."

(41) More a Reverend Jo's story

In the dark passage, Captain's lowest voice charged me with attaching ta reverend Jo as his shadow. I was ta see he did no harm, as he clearly had no ounce a sense a' sea. I should keep Jo in that room till Captain returned. Doc'd be in ta help.

Jo an' Gorden sat in the dingy mess room jawing like best buddies. Seated by the door, I slumped on the table an' feigned sleep. I was gathering questions ta ask Jo, thus keep 'im in the room should he an' Gorden ran low on discussion. I had countless numbers a questions.

"...but I wearied of smithing," Jo was going on. "Business slowed and I tired of cheap customers trying to argue prices. When my father came to visit, he offered that I come take over his church. His health was poorly, and he was growing tired in his older age. Though a tad reluctant, I was finally persuaded.

"We moved in with him and everything went most excellent. Rosie cared so well for Father and I found myself with a fine gift for preaching sermons and making up rules and such. I widely grew a reputation for fine, loud sermons full of fire and brimstone, and the congregation increased as did the collection plate income. I devoted hours to penning sermons. And my parishioners were so happy ta be pointed the righteous pathway, and assisted ta save their sinning souls. Obvious to every eye, me and the pulpit were a match made for heaven.

"Did you see how I snuck that up on you, Jamie? It's a favorite saying I penned. Me and the pulpit were a match made for heaven. I spend much time putting cleverness in each sermon. It keeps my sheep awake and they appreciate it.

"But where was I? Ah yes, things were going along so great and one Sunday morning one of the stellar members of my flock brought into church his cousin Wilfred Jones, who had recently returned after spending an entire year in the American colonies. As a writer, he traveled about the colonies gathering material for books and articles he planned to publish.

"We three talked hours in the church garden. I learned of all the excitement and beauty in the colonies and about the naked heathen natives lingering about in need of religion.

"I won't bother you with details. I wrote it into my week's sermon and soon we all shared the idea. We'd adventure to the colonies to bring our strong religion to the heathen Indians.

"One of our flock had a good Christian uncle, Mister Wiggins, in ownership of this boat. He offered its use quickly at a low price, so we're suddenly on this expedition."

"Where'd ya find this Captain an' crew?" Gorden asked. I crossed that one off the long list a questions in my mind.

"Mister Wiggins knew of Captain Smyth. He's older and looking to retire to the colonies. Sadly he had a drinking problem which Mister Wiggins must a been unaware of."

"Where'd ya get the crew?"

"We gave Smyth money an' he recruited the four crewmen."

"Only four?" Gorden uttered with surprise.

"Yes. We thought we gave him money for more, but he assured us that four was enough, especially since we Christian men were able to join in the work aboard ship.

"But enough talk of me. Tell me about your ship, Jamie. What kind of a vessel was she and how did your Captain lose her in a storm? I'm trying to decide whether I should put at the helm of this ship a Captain who lost his vessel to a storm."

"'Twas a ship much like this, with sails an' such, but smaller. Yet we didn't lose her ta any squall. We got flipped by a wall."

"Don't be daft. There's no walls out about on the ocean. You're joking me," Reverend Jo scoffed.

"'Twas a wall a water, Adam. A wave going up o'er the ship! Sailors call it a wall. I saw it with these two astounded eyes!"

"How strange that I never heard of such. Yet if you witnessed it, Jamie, then I believe it most certainly arises."

"'Tis nature's rare sight, occurring many generations apart. No witness survives, so few men know. Some say 'tis a beauty-full wild child fleeing ugly parents--a strong earth shiver, an' huge squall. Yet others see it as splashup from heavenly debris. 'Tis whispered by sailors as God's hand sweeping cross the sea brushing all crumbs from the table ta the floor."

"What fine imagery," Reverend Jo sighed. "Sailors can do so well with word pictures at times. Would that I might site such a wave someday. Is there a way to know one's scheduled?"

"No, none a' tall, Jo. Ya wouldn't want the view lest ya had a fierce desire ta be a crumb brushed ta the floor."

"How are you seven not crumbs ta the floor then?"

"Captain Werthman's great skill brought us through an' saved our lives. He'd prepared the ship so well that she bobbed up after the wave passed, yet went o'er ta float topsy-turvy. We seven lived an' were trapped aboard."

"Lord. Tell how you escaped?" Reverend Jo beseeched.

"Captain Werthman quick gave birth ta the fine idea a firing off a cannon. Thus we breached the hull an escaped."

"Seems your Captain did well in such a poor situation, yet I didn't think freighters had cannons. This ship has none."

"They were protection from pirates. The *Vengeferth* had six."

"*Vengeferth.* Such a strange name for a freighter."

"Aye, an' *Crazy Cousin's* an odd one as well," Gorden smiled sweetly. "Ya never know how owners'll name 'em these days."

(42) Preparing for a meet up

"Yes, but we two have gone on talking so long, and you haven't seen Rosie yet, nor little Mary. They aren't even aware you're aboard. Ollie, please go and bring them here, but don't tell them why. We want Jamie's presence to be a great surprise for them," Reverend Jo chuckled.

"Aye, but let's consider the condition a this aged *Crazy Cousin,* Adam," Gorden continued.

"Yes this ship's a well-aged vessel. That's why we got her at a good rate. But I've faith she'll get us to the colonies with our prayers and our Lord's fine assistance."

"But Jo, that *extra* water ya pump out isn't really so *extra*."

"Might it be good there, Jamie? How could that be?"

"No. I mean it should never gain entrance ta the ship a' tall. This ship's hull seems ta be leaking pretty bad."

"But all ships leak water. At least when they're older. It's the beast's nature. Mister Wiggins, the owner, told me. It's why they carry pumps. Are you saying he might be wrong on that?"

"Did ya notice how much thick seaweed clings ta the hull?"

"Only on the part below water. Mister Wiggins says he's not cleaned it, as bare knuckles are under there. They shouldn't be bothered as they hold the hull together and stop leaks."

"I'm thinking he might be wrong on that too, Jo."

"Oh, but Wiggins is a good Christian. He's owned ships for many years. He knows about seafaring. You've been sailing but a short while, Jamie. Perhaps he could teach you some things about ships," Reverend Jo patiently explained.

"Likely I've more ta still learn about ships, but--"

'Twas then that Gorden's lovely sister an' wee, bouncy niece brushed past me. Both quickly saw Gorden, an' jumped ta his arms squealing delight. I let on they awoke me.

Doc came in right behind 'em an' stood by me. Whilst they traded their happy hellos, I got 'im out the door ta the dark passageway. There I quickly an' most quietly informed 'im that we'd found Jo dumber'n a watch fob, without half a clue on what he was doing a' sea. He an' I were ta hang tight ta Jo, keeping 'im busy an' out a trouble till the Captain returned.

I reentered with Doc in time ta hear Jo saying, "Yes Rosie, it was surely part of God's great design that we were here to so timely rescue Jamie and his friends. I saw their foundering craft had a huge hole in the bottom and was held up mostly by thin canvas and kegs all around. They clearly would have perished in even the smallest storm had we not come to their rescue. I've offered them refuge on our way to the colonies."

I pulled Jo aside. "Reverend Jo, could this family reunion go up ta the deck," I asked, "whilst we glean from ya a little more valuable information about the ship?"

"Why don't all of us just go up and--"

"No," I urged. "We three must stay put, so's ta be here when Captain Werthman returns from studying the broke pump. He's certain ta need your valuable counsel, Reverend Jo."

"Yes. I'm sure," Jo agreed an' sent Gorden with his joyfull, lovely relatives up on deck ta finish their surprise reunion.

"Now Doc, tell us the *full* condition a Smyth," I asked. I stepped on the word *full* ta remind him go slow an' spend time.

He gave me the glance an' started in, "I checked him out as best I could, and he has problems. His biggest one is a shortage of alcohol. He had a strong habit of often nipping at the bottle until he found himself well locked up in that room."

"Yes," Jo agreed. "We've helped him with his drinking problem. I spent a day in his office, and everywhere I turned, a small bottle fell out. In his room the boys found bottles large and small. I saw his problem and knew we must help him get past it. He now seems through the worst of it."

Captain Werthman strode in with the other men.

"Tell me, Doc, how's the Captain's health?" He asked.

"Smyth's in fair condition, Captain Werthman. He had a serious cold shortly after leaving London. While locked in quarantine, his state worsened due to a lack of alcohol, to which his body's well accustomed. The fact that he was unable to abandon ship with the others of his crew, I believe, worsened his mental condition. Yet he's had time to recover, and his main problem now is a strong terror at being here aboard the *Crazy Cousin*. It's converted him to a man of constant prayer."

"Yes. We've had success steering Captain Smyth to the Christion path," Reverend Jo told. "His life's turned to the much to the better, yet he hasn't found it in him to show gratitude. He's mentally unstable and unable to yet speak calmly with me, but he'll come around soon I'm sure."

"Fine. We've the lay a the land an' 'tis time for a meeting," Captain concluded. "Someone fetch Gorden. Doc, bring up Captain Smyth. Don't dally. Time's wasting."

"Smyth's unsteady." Doc said. "I'm unsure he can make it."

"Tell 'im there's a swig a rum for 'im after the meeting. Ya might see 'im run till ya can't catch up," Captain chuckled.

"I'm so sure that's not a good idea sir--" Reverend Jo began.

"Don't worry, a swig can't hurt when no other follows."

"Truly I feel rum would be a bad idea, yet I speak of him coming here. I've helped him improve his health, but he and I are not yet best friends and he's quite excitable."

"Don't worry Reverend Jo, we'll protect ya," Captain assured. "Men, help Doc restrain Captain Smyth should he be excited."

(43) The meet up starts

Gorden strode in, Captain Smyth behind. Smyth moving as well as Captain Werthman'd suggested. Men had ta grab 'im as he went straight for Reverend Jo. I helped, an' his struggle felt unlike that of a sickly man. His mouth was quite healthy also. It spewed strong language I won't repeat.

Stepping ta Smyth's face, Captain Werthman spoke calm, "Captain Smyth, y'll get no rum lest ya settle down. I'm aware y've not taken a liking ta Reverend Jo, but these men an' myself give 'im our protection. Ya need ta go through us ta get at 'im."

Smyth looked about at us then settled back. "That'd best be ****** good rum, mister," he muttered, an' went silent.

"Fine. Now all sit, an' let's decide what we're each ta do," Captain told, an' all found seats.

"I must learn the measure a the *extra* water in this ship's belly. When'd ya last go down there, Captain Smyth?"

He muttered swear words 'fore spitting, "I don't know."

"Why wouldn't ya know?"

"I've lately been locked up, unable ta tell night from day."

"Reverend Jo, when'd he last go below an' measure?"

"Twenty days ago. It was before we put him in sick bay."

"Captain Smyth, how high was the ship's *extra* water then?"

"Alright, alright, let's speed this up. I'll tell ya what you're looking at here, Captain ah...What was your name, sir?"

"Werthman."

Captain Smyth's eyes went wide, then slowly narrowed, "Captain Werthman. Should a seen it. I've heard a the nose. The great gentleman pirate with magical guns," he sneered.

"Fine Captain Smyth, nice ta meet ya. Now get us back ta the measure a *extra* water your ship carries."

"'Tis his ship. Not mine!" He snarled, glaring at Reverend Jo.

"Fine. We'll set on your gravestone, '*Twasn't my ship.* Now tell...wait. We waste time. Gorden, take one a Reverend Jo's boys ta hold a candle an' try ta fathom repair on the pump."

"Aye, Captain," Gorden went out quick.

"Whatever we do," Captain swore, "we'll put forth our good effort ta revive pump two. Lives appear in the balance."

"Lest we see another ship, you're dead right," Smyth muttered. "A jib on the horizon's been my constant prayer for days. Ta my eyes the pump's beyond any repair we might do a' sea.

Yet bringing it back ta life 'd certainly brighten our future.

"We'll see," Captain went on. "Now that we've turned some attention ta the broke pump, 'tis time ta study this *Crazy Cousin's* situation. Explain the *extra* water, Captain Smyth."

"When we've one pumps going strong, ship's standing still, an' the chop's low, the level goes down," Smyth explained.

"Goes down how fast?"

"Slow."

"What if the ship's moving?" Captain Werthman asked.

"Then, we need two pumps ta hold the water level," Captain Smyth muttered. He was sweating an' gazed down, not looking Captain Werthman ta the eye.

"An' with one pump, Captain Smyth?"

"One pump won't hold the water level if the ship's moving."

"I think we're getting the clear picture," Captain sighed. "I heard both you an' Mister Wiggins told Reverend Jo his flock must keep pumping 'cause if they stopped, the pump mightn't restart. Did ya *really* tell 'im that, Captain Smyth?"

"Aye," Smyth confessed low, eyes down.

"Ta be honest, that was the truth ya told. Yet what ya said was really an old seafarer's joke, wasn't it?"

"Aye," Smyth mumbled yet lower.

"The Captain seems ta be losing his voice here," Captain Werthman spoke loudly slow an' calm. "My crew's heard it, so I'll explain the humor ta the Reverend. Smyth an' Wiggens said your flock mustn't stop pumping, without spelling out *why* the pump mightn't restart. Once stopped, the pump wouldn't restart, Reverend Jo, 'cause even the best pumps can't restart on the ocean's bottom.

(44) The meet up goes on

"Any way ya might disagree on that, Captain Smyth?"

"All we told was true. I warned Reverend Jo well an' loud ta keep pumping. With two pumps, I felt we had a fine chance ta make the trip. I was aboard. My life was wagered as well."

"Ya made *extra* water aboard sound normal an' harmless,"

Captain barked. "An' told half the truth, using an old sailor's joke that'd insult any brain with the least knowledge a ships.

"As for your life being wagered. Where are all the smallboats? Ya sailed with smallboats enough ta save the hides a you an' the crew, yet a flock a o'er forty are stowed aboard. Passenger ships need smallboats for all," Captain growled loud.

"'Twas up ta the owner. Reverend Jo had strong faith," Captain Smyth mumbled.

"When is it not a Captain's duty ta see ta passenger safety? Do ya see us as ignorant know-nothings 'cause we're pirates?"

"I see ya as a pirate Captain who lost his ship ta a squall, which clearly means you're less Captain than your legend boasts," Captain Smyth spat, eager ta turn the conversation.

"If I'd lost her ta the ugliest squall, I'd take your point Smyth, though sounds that ya come so near making light a my many good men an' dear friends who perished with our ship. Yet, on the squall ya suggest took her down, you're sorely misinformed. 'Twas a wall took her down," Captain snarled low.

"Hah!" Smyth scoffed, "Story's a laugh. Ya think me soft in the head as Jo here! None escapes a wall, leastways seven."

 Our seven loud silences sucked away his smile. He studied faces, an' fathomed the grim hardness in every two bloodshot eyes. His own eyes widened. "A wall!" He squeaked. "I heard many ships were late coming in 'fore we set sail, an' we passed none on our way, yet I never considered a wall. How big?!"

"O'er half the horizon wide, near a full ship high," Doc said.

"'Twent up well o'er a ship, Doc," I corrected, flashing in my mind ta the cowering *Daisy Belle*. "Ya went down ta tighten ship, whilst I helped blow off the guns."

"My God. Tell it all!" Captain Smyth gasped. "I must hear how ya met it an' came through."

"DeVoe, tell it short. We've not a year," Captain told.

"We kept a strong hull with no wormholes," I started in. "Captain'd well considered a course a action in a wall's path, an' we had the great good luck ta see an' recognize it early. Whilst others tightened ship, six a us used their kickback ta jettison the deck guns. Their cannonballs cleared away our main mast. Thus lightened, the ship had even weight.

"I gauged the wall's height, 'fore diving down the hatch. My captive eyes saw the monster hover o'er the nearby *Daisy Belle*. Captain shoved me down an' came last. Forty hugged bed legs an' prayed. Our seven prayers were answered."

Silence hung, then Smyth choked out, "May I shake your hand, sir?"

Captain Werthman took his hand. No eye was dry. Particularly Smyth. He was shaken as though he'd been there.

"Back ta this *Crazy Cousin*," Captain went on. "There's a fair amount a food aboard, yet only two kegs a sweetwater. 'Tis dangerously short. Our smallboat saw rain enough ta keep our supply up. Reverend Jo, has your ship found no rain?"

"Rain came twice, but we were unable ta collect much," Reverend Jo told. "First came a squall. The many buckets we put out kept tipping, till we each held one out whilst turning our faces upward with mouths wide. We lost water due to folks falling down, which also caused injuries. Then our second rain was easy and without all the wind and high waves. But it was short enough to only slightly fill all the barrels we set out."

"Rains came, an' ya were unable ta collect much water. Didn't Smyth here tell ya how ta spread canvas an' fill kegs?"

"No. Captain Smyth was beyond sensible words. But we added rain to our prayers, so it'll surely be along directly."

"Ah, 'tis a relief ta know it'll be along directly. Another thing. There's a shortage a line up top. Where's so much a your line, Reverend Jo? I haven't yet seen it stowed aboard."

"During the squall, line came down on our heads, Captain Werthman. It snaked about our feet and folks were stumbling on it. Our hands were busy holding kegs to catch the rainwater, so we kicked the line over the edge."

"Oh Reverend, you're a quick thinker," Captain chuckled.

"Thank you, Captain Werthman." he smiled.

The room being filled with seamen, we all smiled wide.

"You're most welcome. I believe we see the four big problems facing this *Crazy Cousin*. I'm in hope 'tis the total number.

"First problem is a most weak, leaky hull hung heavy with barnacles. 'Tis sad, yet perhaps a grim truth, that the barnacles hold her together whilst they eat her. This problem we a the *Vengeferth* can't assist with. Nothing can be done a' sea.

"Second problem, Reverend Jo, is the second pump is broke. Thus, Captain Smyth has clearly told us, the ship must sit still or sink. Most fortunately two smiths are aboard, myself an' Gorden. We're uncertain, yet hope ta repair the pump. 'Tis a simple mechanism we *should* be able ta mend. Whether we'll find parts an' tools aboard ta do so is yet unclear.

"Other problems are shortages a sweetwater an' line. We're in luck. Our smallboat has kegs a sweetwater. Well Husbanded, they'll hold this ship a time. Our kegs are lashed with the needed line as well. 'Tis time ta go up an' lade the kegs aboard."

(45) Our craft gone, we get ta work

Having told his best news last, Captain had cheered the face a every man but Reverend Jo. Elbows ta the table, he leaned for'rd wearing a grimace, palms o'er his eyes.

"There's a problem, Captain Werthman," he moaned, shaky voice low an hard ta hear. "On my way from the funeral service, I espied your desperate craft and I saw it was useless. Had a big hole in the bottom. I told the boys to bring up your belongings and push it off. Didn't want it banging our hull. There was no need for it. You were safely aboard. I took yours for empty kegs, keeping the vessel afloat. We've many empty kegs."

Surprise widened the Captain's mouth an' paled his face. "All on deck! Eyes ta the horizon!" he roared, an' then ran.

We squinted an' gazed about, scouring the horizon ta no avail. 'Twas gone. Our great small naughts-an'-crosses craft had caught a wave an' journeyed far off whilst we gabbed away. This big, so safe rescue ship had sat still, weighted down by the *extra* water filling her belly.

Captain Werthman begged the whereabouts a the ship's looking glass. Reverend Jo explained he'd insisted on sending it with the crew ta help 'em find their way back ta port. He was sure the new crew'd return with it soon.

Captain pulled Doc, Reed, an' me aside. "Ya two get Reverend Jo's help escorting Smyth ta his room," he explained low. "When ya exit, leave both locked in. 'Tis too bad ya lack laudanum for 'em, Doc. Suggest they practice praying together. We'll clearly need prayers ta set foot a' land again. Harm coming ta either man'll be charged against the other. Remind Smyth how much he enjoys carrying ten fingers. I'll be by ta check on 'em. Step lively. Then join us at the broke pump."

Reverend Jo was glad ta help wrestle Captain Smyth ta his room, but most loudly unhappy ta be left inside when we went out an' locked the door. Doc spelled out Captain's messages through the locked door. For the moment, they were silent. We listened at the door a second, our heads shaking. Then we hurried ta the broke pump.

Gorden spoke, "...measured 'em, an' the gears on neither winch'll fit the pump. Teeth won't match. Yet two matching gears from the small winch, soundly worked in, 'll do the job."

"But can we soundly rework the gears in?" Captain asked.

"It'll take time, an' depend on finding the right wood ta mount the gears," Gorden offered. "There's much wood aboard ta consider, all but the hull. We must choose carefully."

Gorden went ta fetch the winch gears. Captain turned ta searching out the needed wood. Others scoured the ship for tools ta use. Doc an' me looked in on the working pump.

A single candle dimly showed a man an' woman working the pump in the small room. They looked tired an' were working it less than hard an' fast. The woman was Gorden's sister Rosie. She stepped away, an' I took her place at the pump, whilst Doc spoke with her. We men picked up the pump's speed a tad. I could feel 'twould be a tiresome job if done at length.

"How's it going down here?" Doc asked, putting his arm 'round Rosie's shoulders with a smile in his easy fatherly way. She sagged her thin frame, clearly bone weary.

"Going quite well," she answered, catching her breath. "Do

you know my husband's whereabouts?"

"Yes," Doc replied, an' after a breath's pause, went on. "He's in Captain Smyth's room helping 'im in his praying."

"With Captain Smyth?" she gasped, her hand ta her mouth.

"The two are reconciled," Doc smiled. I hoped he spoke near the truth. "Tell me the work schedule for this pump."

"We've matched each man with a woman or older child, and the teams are set for one hour turns," she answered.

"We must adjust that. Match a strong man with a weaker one or an older boy. Give teams half hour turns. It should step up the pace. Add six of us to your list. I'll write the names. Add in a few of the stronger women. Could you set that up?"

"I'll ask my husband about it," Rosie answered.

"No. Reverend Jo's busy saving Captain Smyth's suffering soul. It's clearly the way he should be occupied. Your husband may be able to navigate life on land, yet he's clearly worse than lost at sea. I'm sure you have members of the flock in need of doctoring. I'll go about with you and see to their ills after you adjust the pump schedule. Make the list and give women turns watching the hourglass. They'll fetch men when their turns come due on the pump. That way the pump won't slow."

"Must we pump out the extra water so fast?" Rosie asked.

"That *extra* water is more *extra* than you see," Doc gravely explained. "It comes through a weak hull, an' it's deadly serious. If the ship drinks it in faster than we spit it out, the water wins and we're lost. It appears there's a good chance we'll fix the second pump and then be able to sail back to London. We need pumps doing their best every minute. Don't leave Mister DeVoe working the pump long. He's a bit old for it."

Doc was right. My back was soring up, an' I wheezed.

Rosie heard the seriousness in Doc's voice. No more questions. She wrote a new schedule for the pump work.

(46) Science, the devil's work

I was laboring, so Doc took my place. He pumped, an' gave directions, "We've no need for a water shortage, Wil. Time to work on the problem. Search out, with Reed, six or eightfoot of pipe or hose. Skinnier 'd be better. Don't take any used by a pump. All else is fair game, but for privy drains. Put it in the galley, and fetch a tall, lidded keg to the galley as well.

Then stand the keg up and bore a hole in its side by the middle. A hole to fit the pipe or hose. If I'm still tending to the ill when you progress that far, send Reed for more instruction.

I had no notion what we were working on, but Reed an' me bustled 'round as Doc instructed. 'Twas good ta be busy. Doc, the one forever reading science books, clearly he knew what we were doing. We found the needed hose in the ship's bowels. 'Twas clean an' far from the pumps, so we felt safe on it.

In the galley we two carved on the keg, digging the hole Doc described. We used sharp galley knives. Reed headed out ta ask Doc what's next, but met 'im coming in. Behind Doc an' Reed, came two young women aiming ta begin cooking food.

"Stored bread and cheese must do tonight," Doc told. "We'll soon be using the stove to turn salt water into sweetwater."

"You can do that?" the girls together asked, quite surprised.

"It would be delightfull magic!" the tall girl laughed lightly.

"Yes. You'll see soon. It's science," Doc assured 'em. "Once we get it started, we'll need the women's help keeping it going all night. Should be a keg filled by morning, maybe sooner."

"Science?" The younger girl gasped. "The devil's work. We can't help on that." The two backed out an' hurried off.

"Wonderfull. Science is the devil's work!" Doc bemoaned. "I chose a bad word. Where was my mind? If I agree it's magic, they'll help. I should have known not to use the word."

Captain Werthman darkened the door an', hearing Doc's last words, asked, "How goes the work, Doc? What word shouldn't ya say? I hope ya used no nasty swear words. Clearly when the women hear bad language, they become a stirred up bee's nest. We might find ourselves returned home ta send out another imaginary crew ta save this bloody sinking ship."

We all chuckled, an' then explained ta 'im that *science* was a swear word aboard this ship. He gave that a short, unhumorous laugh, then we exchanged information less foolish.

Doc told, "As to what we're doing, we're setting this up to change sea water to sweetwater. It's going fine. I expect we'll get started in an hour. How are the pump repairs going?"

"We can turn sea water ta sweetwater, Doc?" Captain asked.

"My science books say we boil water on the stove and run the steam down a hose to the keg. Little salt goes with the steam, so we'll ladle water from the keg with little salt."

"How fast can we fill a keg?"

"I'm unsure. The hose should drip at a good pace. Steam getting through the hose 'll form drops in the keg on the sides. It'll drip down. We must keep the heat up, add salt water to the pot, and ladle sweetwater from the keg. Wet cloth wrapped on the hose ta cool it, should speed things up."

"Clearly ya got it figured, Doc. Y'll have the women's help soon. The work on the broke pump's going well. We found strong spokes from the helm well suited ta the job. Reed an' Gorden are fashioning 'em ta fit the winch gears. 'Tis slow, carefull work, yet near certain ta be successfull.

"Mister DeVoe, if ya care ta step along, let's enter the animal cage an' see if we can sort things out with Reverend Jo," Captain suggested. As we walked, he went on, "I'm hoping neither he nor Smyth has seriously injured the other. I little enjoy separating men from their fingers, but I'm a man a my word."

(47) Smyth an' Jo

Captain an' me were encouraged by the silence we found at their door. Then we were confounded ta see 'em on their beds, both asleep, none the worse for wear. The two stirred as we entered. They slowly sat up, as though they'd shared the same sleep. It felt ta be a child's nursery at the end a nap time.

Upon seeing Captain Werthman's face, Smyth started in, "Rum! What the devil happened ta my rum, Werthman? I took ya as a man a yer word. Did I *mis*took ya as a man a yer word?"

"'Tis *Captain* Werthman ta ya sir. I wonder where ya figure I'd get rum on this ocean after weeks aboard a smallboat. Ya seem ta think all pirates spend their days carrying 'round rum ta stay stinking drunk, which makes ya as daft as a man who'd hire a half sunk coffin ta voyage the ocean.

"As for my word, I didn't say *when* after the meeting y'd get rum, Smyth. I *am* a man a my word. Y'll taste rum when ya set foot on dry land. Be silent whilst I speak with Reverend Jo."

Reverend Jo jumped in, "Captain Werthman, why am I captive aboard my own ship? As the owner I demand—"

"Don't go demanding, Reverend Jo," Captain Werthman cut 'im off sharp. "Ya freely relieved me a my boat, so I'm now freely relieving ya a yours. Even up. Square deal. 'Tis the poorer bargain for me. I had a seaworthy craft an' twenty kegs a drinking water for seven men. Your ship has a wormhole-weak hull, broke pump, shortage a line ta hang sails, an' two kegs a drinking water for fifty people. The *Crazy Cousin's* no bargain. 'Tis more of a tragedy most near its ending.

"I didn't decide on our trade though. 'Twas more you. Ya decided when your foolishness pushed off my boat unasked. Y've pushed off my only means ta escape this foundering coffin. So the only path left ta me is an attempt at saving this desperate ship. Being the only choice available, 'tis made.

"If ya have more arguments on it Reverend Jo, give 'em now."

"I demand the now sober Captain Smyth here--"

"Fine, Reverend," Captain cut 'im off. "Let's ask Captain Smyth a few more questions.

"We'll go at it backwards, Captain Smyth. First, tell us the chances a crew in any boat'd have a finding us, were they ta set sail any place, ooooh let's just say London."

Silence was thick in the candle light. Neither Captain spoke, just stared in the other's eyes. Captain Werthman sat steady, hard, an' calm. A drop a sweat fell off his large nose. Smyth's upper lip twitched. His squirming hands wouldn't stay still. Smyth's teeth were grinding his jaw, chewing back words.

Captain Werthman demanded, "Give a number Captain. What's your best estimate at the odds?"

More silence full a teeth grinding, an' Smyth spat, "Naught."

"Dead on, Captain. I couldn't a spoke it better. Now, how clearly would any sailing man see those odds?"

Another silence, an' Smyth grunted, "Hundred percent."

"On the nose again. 'Twould be easily seen as a dead fool's mission by any sailing man. Tell us what chance there is that a crew might be found willing ta set out on such a fool's mission, lest they were the lost folk's near family."

"Naught, naught, naught," he spoke slowly, each repetition lower, hands o'er ears, laying back, an' rolling ta face the wall.

"Reverend Jo, recall that Smyth recently stated this ship's working pump can't keep down the *extra* water leaking in, if the chop's high or the ship's moving," Captain hesitated a bit. "Have ya a clear picture a the situation ya had when my crew an' me arrived? The situation Captain Smyth put ya in."

Reverend Jo's mind was churning. He sputtered words of several sentences, each utterance muttering down ta nothing.

"Whilst your flock prayed for a replacement crew, Captain Smyth's only prayer was for a surprise sail on the horizon. He knew 'twas your only hope, a hope erased by the wall a water ya unknowingly sailed out right behind. 'Twas a wall which we seven survived, yet had swept the ocean clean a ships.

"'Tis time ya saw us pirates as God's answer ta your prayers, Reverend Jo. We were uninformed a any such plan, yet can't deny the possibility. In turn, your foundering ship must be the answer ta our prayers. Consider how, in this huge empty ocean, our barely moving crafts found each other like two tiny needles in this world's largest haymow. What's that but a miracle?"

Reverend Jo's head rocking up an' down, he repeated, "Yes." eyes closed, as though peaceably jawing with his Lord.

(48) Smyth comes out, Jo stays

"Fine, Reverend Jo. My men are at work turning this ship around ta a sailable vessel. Our success isn't quite certain. Second pump seems repairable an'--"

"The Lord will assist," Reverend Jo warmly assured, reaching out ta pat Captain Werthman's hand.

"I'm certain He'll assist," Captain Werthman nodded. "But we may also need a small assist from you, Reverend Jo."

"From me? Seems I'm more hindrance than assistance at sea, Captain Werthman."

"Your self-measure 'tis encouraging. Yet we've a problem which I feel, with some effort, ya might solve. In the galley we plan ta turn ocean water ta sweetwater--"

"You can do that?" Reverend Jo's surprise interrupted.

"Yes. 'Tis science. Doc's knowledge. We'll need the women's help ta boil water an' collect it back without salt. Now--"

"Sounds most unnatural, Captain. Only the Lord changes water. He turns it to fine wine," Reverend Jo explained.

"Oh, so 'tis unnatural," Captain Werthman repeated. "Is all done in the name a science unnatural, sir?"

"Most. Science is the devil's work against the church. Every answer a man needs is found on the bible's beautyfull page."

"So 'tis no unnatural science in the pump we're repairing?"

"That's just a pump. There's no unnatural science in a pump. Folks work it, and it moves water," Reverend Jo explained.

"It makes water flow upward. Where in nature is it natural for water ta flow upward?"

"I'm certain it flows upward naturally from some wells."

"Fine. 'Twill be night soon, an' God's likely ta spread a thousand wondrous stars across the sky. I may sit back an' spend this night enjoying the sight, or I might use the *unnatural* science instruments in the Captains quarters ta measure those stars, thus chart our way home. Which would ya prefer?"

"No. We need but God's glorious northern star and our naked eye to be guided safely home," Reverend Jo smiled.

"Care ta comment on that, Captain Smyth?"

Smyth mumbled ta the wall, "We're lost with no maps or instruments. North Star's but half the answer."

"Reverend," Captain Werthman went on, "God put stars up there an' gave us good minds ta read their message pointing the way home. 'Tis His handwriting. We can read His message in the stars, or we can stumble lost in the dark. 'Tis far more certain God wrote the message in the stars than 'tis that He had the least ta do with writing your bible.

"We might argue this all night, but I must return ta the work a getting this ship going. A thing ya may consider is that your beautyfull wife an' precious young daughter need potable water, as do your flock an' my crew. We'd own twenty kegs more a sweetwater but for your stupidity in pushing my boat off. Ya also recently chased raindrops 'round the deck with open mouth, whilst Captain Smyth below could a showed ya the way ta husband kegs a rainwater.

"Seems God's been sending ya water every way He knows, Reverend, whilst' ya busied yourself throwing it away. In the galley, God may offer a last chance. Don't throw it away.

"But I'm thinking on a way past this, Reverend Jo. DeVoe an' Smyth lack strong backs for pumping. I saw 'em as fishing with the children for food, whilst the women made sweetwater. There's no reason Devoe an' Smyth can't work the galley. Yourself an' your flock can catch fish. Jesus, 'imself, fed fish ta the multitudes, an' I've heard He might a been a fisherman a' times. Catching fish *can't* be unnatural.

"How about ya, Captain Smyth? Seems you're highly needed in the galley. Your grievous mistake put these folks here in great peril, yet a late I've been told we're better than our worst mistake. Perhaps 'tis true for us both. Ta my mind, ya get a start at redeeming yourself in this, though I must point out 'tis only in my mind. Unlike Reverend Jo, I claim no ability ta fathom our Lord's thoughts or intentions."

Captain Smyth sat up slow, "It seems a chance ta help save my worthless hide. When there's no rum ta be had, I enjoy a drink a water, an' I've no wish ta die for the lack of it. As ta my sorry soul, 'twill likely need far more work ta avoid hell. Time wastes. Enough jawing. Let's begin."

"An' how about yourself, Reverend Jo?" Captain Werthman asked, his voice lightened. "I expect from ya the largest catch."

"But I've never fished before. I don't know how t--"

"So much the better. Y'll get all the beginner's luck. 'Tis near dusk. Can't see what you're catching at night. Ya get a hook out first thing in the morn. Y've *eaten* fish 'fore, right?"

"Yes. Less often than I'd like," Reverend Jo's voice, like the Captain's, lightened. "What kind of fish are caught out here?"

"Mostly sharks. We don't hoist big ones. Though as tasty, they're a danger ta bring aboard. An' ya can't haul 'em up 'fore their teeth cut the line. We get plenty a small ones ta feed us."

"Captain, **sharks**?! Sharks aren't eaten. It's most unnat--"

"**No**!" Captain shot back. "I'll **not** hear the bloody word from your lips once more t'day, lest I hurt my hard fist breaking your nose till it swells up big an' **unnatural** as my own!"

Reverend Jo neither spoke nor met the Captain's eye. I didn't hide a small smile at the Captains words. The light was weak an' none looked at me. Smyth's hand hid his smile.

"Reverend Jo, your ignorance weighs down this ship, trying so hard ta sink us. For everyone's safety, ya stay here an' speak ta none but DeVoe till we reach land. He'll deliver your water an' food. Ya needn't drink any *unnatural* water or eat nicely cooked *unnatural* shark's meat. Just send 'em back."

Me an' Captain Smyth followed Captain Werthman. He locked the door, handed me the key, an spoke loudly near the door, "He's ta speak with none, DeVoe, lest he utter more ignorance certain ta endanger the ship."

(49) He's dithers

As we strode ta see the pump repairs, I pointed out that we had little line ta hang sails, so 'twould be a slow trip an' asked, "Captain do ya mean ta keep the dolt away from all aboard, including Rosie, all the way ta London?" An' I offered in humor, "If ya can excuse my expression Captain, it seems that keeping husband an' wife apart so long 'd be *unnatural*."

"Aye, *'tis unnatural*," he chuckled. "We'll talk with Rosie an' learn how far she's a the same bent as Jo. Luckily women aren't oft so foolish. Unfortunately, so many *men* a this world *are*."

Smyth spoke up, "Captain, did I mishear? Are ya expecting ta repair the pump? I worked on pumps a' times, an' fully expected ta repair these if need be. Yet I saw no way ta mend this one's broken gear a' sea."

"There's no smithing tools aboard for us ta work metal, so my men are busy trading in two matching gears from the small winch. Appears it'll do just fine. Should be done soon."

"*Two matching gears!* Marvelous. A course it'll do if ya work it right. I should a seen it myself. Y've two smiths aboard?"

"Aye, two."

"Two smiths an' a fine Doc. Ya turn my mind on pirates, Captain, though I doubt many crews are a your cut."

Captain Smyth was excited out a his skin by the work on the second pump. Better than most aboard, he knew our so slim chance a survival with one pump. His excitement I understood.

We looked in ta find the pump repair going well. Reed could finish the slow work. Captain sent Smyth ta the galley, whilst he an' I took Gorden ta find Rosie. On the way we stopped an' Captain filled Gorden in on Reverend Jo.

"He's dithers, Gorden! Dumber 'n a keg a nails. Saved no rain! His flock ran about with mouths open whilst kicking out line needed ta hang sails. Taking salt from water's unnatural, an' eating shark meat as well. Both a which his flock, wife, an' small Mary need ta survive. *Unnatural's* his favorite word. The size a his ignorance is the *most* unnatural thing aboard!"

"Aye, I never found 'im ta be the sharpest nail whilst showing 'im smithing," Gorden nodded. "He had neither the quickest nor slowest mind, yet saw 'imself clever, an' oft thought he saw a better way. I'd a tried ta warn Rosie on 'im, yet love's well known ta be deaf. A' land he gets by, whilst a' sea he piles mistake atop error. He's well intentioned though. In his church he's found his calling, making up rules an' sermons. Clearly u*nnatural* must show itself oft in those sermons.

"But what about Rosie?" Captain turned ta ask. "How far is your sister in his *unnatural* set a mind?"

"I'm unsure. We've been apart years. She's still taken by Jo, yet Rosie was a lively one in school, an' of a practical mind."

"I hope she's now of a practical mind. We'll need women's

help on food an' water, whilst men work two pumps."

We found Rosie resting, with beautyfull little Mary asleep in her arms. Though not unclean, the living space was dark an' poor. The folks 'd moved kegs a stored goods ta set out each family's living space, yet kegs couldn't be stacked high, as they'd fall in a high chop. The *Crazy Cousin* was a freighter, unmeant for any passenger comforts.

So's not ta wake the child, Captain spoke soft, "Gorden, can ya hold your lovely niece whilst we show Rosie ta the galley?"

Gorden was eager ta hold the child an' Rosie glad ta give her o'er. Away from the sleeping child, she asked, "Captain Werthman, you took the women from the pumps and out of the kitchen as well. What are we to do? We can't just sit fretting." She appeared so weary an' frail, yet spoke strong a spirit.

"I'm sorry. We need the men's strength on the pumps."

"Can men pump with no cooked food in their bellies?"

"Ya don't know how tempting that is ta men who've not tasted cooked morsels for months. But please step ta the galley. 'Tis where we dearly need the women's help right now."

(50) Another meet up

We'd an o'erfull boatload a worry. On a wide sea, we clung ta an old ship with a miserable weak hull, little water, an' no smallboats. 'Twas a poor wager our *Crazy Cousin'd* weather the next squall. She mightn't fully cave. Yet should she open wide enough ta gulp in more water 'n two pumps could spit out, we'd swim with the sharks. Hulls might be repaired a' sea, but no chance on a ship as old an' weak as the *Crazy Cousin*.

'Neath the weight a that worry, the men's aching bloody hands worked two pumps days, an' one a' night. We crawled our way slowly along. The weather held, as did the rotten hull.

Smyth an' the women had potable water flowing from the galley. Ten a our smaller barrels were full when, six days on, a joyfully welcomed easy rain rolled in near dusk. 'Twas greeted by much cheer an' laughter, but no running about the deck chasing raindrops. We quick showed Reverend Jo's flock how ta spread canvas an' catch runoff. When every empty keg aboard was topped off, we emptied the kegs we'd filled in the galley an' refilled 'em with the sweeter rainwater.

Our potable water worries gone, we hastened ta clear out the galley. The women meant ta cook a hearty mess the next morn. We were weak-kneed with exhaustion, yet late eve, Captain sent me about rousting the men for a meet up. 'Twas ta be us seven crew an' Reverend Jo. I came inta the mess room last with Jo. Flickering candles showed bloodshot, bleary eyes an' gaunt faces such as I'd seen aboard the o'rturned *Vengeferth*.

"I know we're tired," Captain Werthman started in lowly, offering up the bloody obvious, "but things need jawing on."

"Where's Captain Smyth?" Reverend Jo piped up.

"He's uninvited cause he's needs discussing. Ya brought 'im up, so let's consider first if an' when we hang the scoundrel."

"**Hang** him!" Jo croaked. "Why do that? He seems to have turned to a fine fellow. What's he done?"

"Aye, he's been a fine mate a late. But 'tis not his truest colors. I remind ya, the bloke set sail with ya in a sinking ship that had only smallboats enough for the crew," Captain explained. "I'm sure the owner promised 'im part a the ship's insurance money as well. Ships lost a' sea put good insurance money in owners' pockets, whilst those sunk a' harbor bring little. It added up ta Wiggins an' Smyth drowning ya an' your flock like a grain sack full a unwanted pups."

"But we didn't die. So he's no murderer," Jo argued.

"*Attempted* murder then. An' we're still in trouble, Reverend Jo. One good squall an' we may well be tasty shark meat."

"But if we go down, Smyth'll go too. There's no need hanging him. When we reach London, he may go on trial and you'll be great heroes for saving us," Reverend reasoned.

"You don't consider we're pirates," Captain told in the low candle light. "A' land, we'll seek the least attention. We feel good about saving your flock, but escaping with our hides is the only reward we ask. What do the rest a ya think on Smyth?"

"We're all better 'n our worst mistake," Gorden offered.

"Aye," Captain nodded. "Yet attempted murder a that many children an' women is a lot a mistake ta let pass. An' I doubt 'tis his first or worst mistake? A wretch who'd stoop so low as ta sign on an' captain this sinking ship, likely was a slaver."

A short silence, an' Dessinger avowed, "Makes sense. Let's string 'im up now, so's the kids an' women aren't bothered."

"We'll let on he went o'er the rail," Heitman agreed.

"No, no. Wait," Reverend Jo came in. "You can't hang a man on suspicion. Maybe he thought we had a good chance to reach the colonies. And we don't know he was a slaver. Slaving is yet legal in some places. In the bible--"

"I know what your bible says on slaving," Captain spat. "'Tis another problem I have with the bloody book. We took slaving ships a' times. Wouldn't stow animals in such condition. Even swine. I wished ta hang Captain an' crew on the stinking ships. Yet hanging 'em meant leaving a foundering ship. Slaves know less 'n nothing about ships. They'd die a poor an' certain death. So we took fingers from Captain an' all crewmen. Let 'em know they'd lose hands or arms should we meet 'em again an' find their cargo in such a sordid state.

"Aboard one slaving ship we had the fortune ta find a slave able ta speak some few words a the King's English. He chose two friends an' we saved the three. Our *Vengeferth* hadn't the room ta save all the miserables. In six months those three spoke passable English. They became some a the best crewmen aboard. In the next days I aim ta get a fix on whether Smyth was a slaver. We'll then reconsider his fate."

"Captain, you've navigated with instruments a few nights. How far out are we are from London?" Reverend Jo asked.

"I'd say two weeks, riding the main sail at this snail's pace.

"I mainly called ya men in ta suggest 'tis time ta face another dire problem. Without smallboats, we're in grave peril. Ya all clearly see any squall could put this ship down. We were so lucky to get easy rain with no high chop. With much potable water aboard, now 'tis time ta quickly fashion some rafts."

"Can we make rafts strong enough ta face a squall?" I asked.

"May depend on the squall. We'll do our best with what's at hand. We're riding the main sail, so all other line can be used. If need be, we'll cut some sails in strips, then twist an' weave the strips inta rope. I saw a keg a nails in the pump room."

(51) Rafts built an' used

Clearly the Captain had the right idea, so the next morn we turned ta fashioning rafts on the deck. Reverend Jo finally had a way ta keep busy that wasn't *unnatural.* Captain let 'im out an' charged 'im with assisting me. Reed, Doc, Gorden, an' me, each had our raft ta build. Captain supervised the wood gathering, so no lubber might tear wood from the hull an' sink us. Oliver, Edward, an' many a the women helped gather wood. Some a the women busied themselves cooking food.

In a heavy morn mist, Reverend Jo an' me were first ta start. 'Twas scary thinking a squalls whilst in a mist that'd hide any that might approach. Yet, lacking rafts, what might we do should we espy one? Only drop the sail, tighten ship, an' pray. Yet we'd survived this long without squalls or smallboats.

The inside walls a the ship had much wood ta use. We'd nail it together inta platform beds, then tie on kegs at the corners. I explained it all ta Jo as we went, "Kegs are tied on. Can't nail 'em. Nails crack the wood, an' the kegs lose their seal."

I went on ta tell how we must have all souls tied on safe. He saw the need for that. We'd use the rafts in a high chop, an' clinging ta 'em 'd be a frightfull chore.

A course the reverend got it all wrongheaded. Whilst helping nail together our raft, he offered, "We'll tie the folks to the middle of the raft and they can hang tight to each other, then line the rafts near together so they can help each other."

"Not quite. Ya haven't seen the height a the waves we might ride out," I explained, hammering a nail. "Consider how that setup ya described might work should a craft flip. The likely event would leave poor souls, tied ta the middle, trapped beneath, an' soon dead. Any soul so lucky as ta get aloose from under, would be swept out away an' quick lost.

"The rafts are best far apart as well. Nearby they're each other's biggest enemy, sliding o'er, or landing atop each other."

"It seems so clear, Devoe. How's the best way to set it up?"

"We'll be near a dozen on each raft, three or four tied on at each edge. Lines from each soul's waist ta the raft's edge'll be just long enough for 'im ta sit in the middle. All facing outward in a circle, arms locked. Whichever way she tilts, three or four lines'll hold all ta the middle. We'll put blocks on the raft ta brace feet as well. Should a raft flip, first soul ta climb atop helps pull the others up, till we're all back atop the raft clinging together in the middle. It'll be far from easy in a mean squall, but 'tis our best an' only chance."

"Sounds most frightening," Jo choked, his voice atremble.

"Truly. Even more so for one in a cumbersome brown robe. Such garb's unswimable in. It'd quickly grow heavy, an' pull 'im down," I told o'er my shoulder, whilst hammering a nail. "Should the raft flip, no chance he'd be first ta clamber atop."

'Twas my last sight a his robe.

Oliver, Edward, an' all kept bringing wood, till about noon our raft was set. Others were near finished. We lashed kegs ta corners, an' 'twas time ta put her o'er the rail. We'd disabled the small winch, but the big one was ready for the job.

"Devoe, let's leave the rafts on deck to float away if the ship sinks. That way they'll be much easier to board," Jo suggested, as we prepared ta winch her o'er the side.

"That'd do fine if the ship sinks slow, Reverend Jo. Yet if she goes down quick, she sucks the rafts down with her. Which makes this morn a sad waste a sweat."

"Devoe, you have it all figured out, so I'm sure there's a reason we're lowering this raft with empty kegs, when you mentioned we'd half fill 'em with food an' water."

"Heavier kegs mightn't stay tied on whilst we winch her down, Jo. Half filling the barrels is the next step."

After a silence, the reverend bemoaned, "I get it wrong here a' sea every time, Devoe. It's pityfull. I didn't even see the way to put out canvas and catch rain my flock desperately needed."

"I think ya might a got it half right pushing off our smallboat, Jo. The poking out masts could a breached *Crazy Cousin's* hull. A breach at her waterline an' we'd be shark food. We should a winched our smallboat aboard. No, we rushed aboard, then foolishly sat 'round jawing whilst our lives would a been hanging by a thread, had ya not pushed off our craft.

"See, you're a land lubber, Jo. *Most* land lubbers are useless on the briny. Here, you're twice bumfuggled, as the Good Book ya live in says naught on seafaring. Ya flatter me ta suggest I own the mind ta fashion this raft. Seems I've gone on like I found the ideas in my head, but not so. Last night we crew stayed after the meeting jawing on the design a these rafts. Captain, Doc, an' Gorden had the most ideas. Ya see, surviving a' sea is a thinking game. Captain Werthman, Doc, an' Gorden are the chess players a the world. Us others are lucky ta play a fair game a naughts an' crosses.

Surely the reverend 'd not learn I play a fair chess game.

Reverend Jo frowned, an' gave a less 'n loud grunt in agreement, "Yes, but I don't know Gorden to play chess."

"Right, but when he goes to it, he'll have it in a minute. We two might pick it up in months, yet never be so good."

After a sizable silence, whilst we lowered our raft, Reverend Jo changed the subject, asking, "What are the odds we'll use this raft, Devoe. Riding out a storm on it scares me."

"Puts fear in me as well. 'Twould be no fun. Clear ta any seaman's eye, a squall's likely ta send this *Crazy Cousin* down. Yet no squall's in the offing. 'Twill be a less worrisome ride back ta port with four rafts tied on behind though. An' we'll be glad ta have 'em when we find London an' fancy going ashore."

"London'll be a fine sight. We'll celebrate, praise the Lord."

"Amen ta that. Though I'm doubting there'll be many 'round ta celebrate with ya. The wall that took our *Vengeferth*, musta swept the sea clean such that few ships've arrived a late. Y'll get much attention when the word gets out about ya though."

"You sound like you don't expect to be with us."

"We'll all go rafting in ta the docks together at dusk, but us seven won't stay 'round ta celebrate. Seems the *Vengeferth's* crew went down with her. Too bad ya never layed eyes on 'em, or met the fine, handsome blokes. I'll explain ta Smyth. Please lay it out ta your flock. 'Tis the only payment we ask."

He nodded, "It's a wage well earned."

I went on ta explain, "For a day Smyth'll be a hero. He fixed *Crazy Cousin's* broke pump, an' steered the way home, steady at the helm. He won't play the hero long. With nobody working her pumps, the *Crazy Cousin'll* go quick. Smyth knows. Soon after, they'll search 'im out ta ask why he set sail with ya in such a ship. He'll slink away an' vanish. If he's meted out punishment for his sins, 'twill be by the Lord.

"As for the ship's owner, I'd expect ya ta get from 'im all your expenses an' more. 'Fore we came aboard, one a your boys fell off the riggin an' died, as I recall. Owner's responsible. Tell the story, an' he should go ta prison, lest he has friends high up."

The weather kept holding, as did the *Crazy Cousin's* weak hull. We eased up the Thames, an' ta the cheers a all aboard, we soon espied the London skyline. 'Twas past noon on a rain dreary day. Yet the sun shone bright aboard the *Crazy Cousin*.

We got out oars we'd fashioned, an' put all souls aboard the four rafts. Water was smooth. A woman began singing Amazing Grace in a prayerfull way, an' soon all joined in. Sun was down when we rowed our way in. Only souls about were boys fishing on the next wharf. They came around ta ask who we were, as our last man climbed up. The flock took ta laughing loud an' talking, going teary eyed with joy. Many knelt ta kiss the dock. We crew a the *Vengeferth* quietly slunk away on a walk-about. An hour along we slipped inta a pub ta find in its back room the most heavenly pints a ale a bloke ever quaffed.

(52) Captain Werthman's tale

Weight finally lifted from our shoulders. We talked, laughed loud, an' drank. In that lowly lit back room, empty but for us seven at the middle table, we finally wheedled from our Captain Werthman the tale a his misspent youth, an' how he came by our now lost, deadly accurate cannons.

"'Tis the time ta let it spill," I chided o'er a pint, whilst we awaited our requested feast. "Ya once suggested y'd give up the tale o'er a fine feast, sir, an' 'tis the picture we see."

"Aye, Captain, ya held out long enough," Doc pestered, whilst others laughed an' chirped in, like so many flocking birds. I was uncertain how much a Captain's story Doc knew. Ta my ear, his voice half suggested he was giving the Captain permission ta tell the tale.

"Fine, fine then. I'm full ready for the telling, men," he chuckled. "Yet 'twill wait till food fills the table an' the door's bolted, thus leaving out the serving folk's ears."

An' so we quaffed an' waited. Then, with the feast on the table, our Captain put us off more. He insisted on a few eating minutes 'fore he started in. None grumbled the least. Savory smells filling the room so heavenly that even the King's story might take a back bench an' wait.

"Aye, men," Captain stood an' started in after much most unmannerly consumption all 'round, "I'd like ta say I was born at age ten. It would be a half truth. Age ten was when I feel the real me showed. My earliest years are a deep shame. 'Tis one a the reasons I put off the tale.

"Like Gorden's father, mine was a smith, yet with a hardness a disposition. A bullying man with smithing arms none'd argue against. A stranger came ta town bent on owning a smithing shop in competition. He was buried with no name by the church. Yet witnesses agree 'twas a fair fight, no weapons.

"But Dad was a skilled smith. An' he never hit Mom, even when he was oft unsober. Us two boys usually deserved what we got. Yet Mom made nary a decision. His was the final word. She knew not ta question. When we boys questioned, we got welts slow ta heal. Yet seldom about the face.

"Seeing Dad's hard ways as fine, I took after 'im. Davy, two years younger, had little choice. Followed my lead. We weren't the biggest lads about, yet proud ta be the feistiest.

"Mom did get her way on one thing. 'Twas our schooling. He

didn't oppose it so strong though. If he did, it mightn't a been. School months ran December first ta mid-March, harvest ta Spring planting. This young dunderhead valued it none an' acted most poorly day ta day, year ta year. At age ten, the nearer small school forced me an' Davy out ta the far city school, two years early. Dad was angered an' opposed. As were we two boys. Mom stood Oak Tree strong against us three. Lord, where an' who'd I be but for her huge strength? I ask it with teared eyes.

"I'll say I got along poorly with fine schoolmasters an' some poorer ones as well. They likely passed me on so's ta be rid a my bother. Then a schoolmaster turned me around.

"Davy an' me hitched up the buggy early an' bounced along an hour's trip ta our new school. 'Twas half dark as we started, but the horse was good. Dad knew horses. First morn I saw we'd arrive covered with kicked up mud when the rain came. Clearly 'twould oft give us our excuse ta skip out.

"Into a classroom a twenty strangers, all boys, I saw step a young schoolmaster. He was but a handfull a years my senior, more muscled, yet little taller'n me, the youngest an' shortest there. Hung his name ta the podium, Mister Fisher."

Hearing the name, I looked ta Doc. He wore a low smile.

"In a classroom a friends at my old school, I'd a laughed." Captain went on. "He was all business. Knew his stuff. Spent the morn asking questions in every area, ta glean where each boy's knowledge was. Yet he put questions in a fine, easy manner as I'd never heard from a schoolmaster. I got no feeling he was up there looking down on us.

He had us tell our stories as well. Last ta speak, I told what a skilled smith Dad was an' how Mom stood strong on sending Davy an' me ta this school. The other boys had better stories.

"Morn flew by, till he dismissed us ta lunch. He asked me ta stay. I was curious, yet not fearfull. I'd had no time nor means ta make my usual trouble. He seemed not the least scarefull.

"*Mister Werthman,*" he started in. "*I'd like someone to play chess with during lunch hours. Would you like to try it?*"

"I, I, I," I stuttered, "*I don't know the game. Why ask me?*"

"None of the boys know the game. I gauge you the smartest, so I'm asking you first. I think you might pick it up quickly and enjoy it. In time, you might play well. Should any of the other boys show interest, you could help me teach them the game."

"I was taken aback. I glanced about the classroom. Did he speak ta me? I'd never been accused a being smart in all my days. Well, by my Mom for sure, yet most particularly not by a schoolmaster. Most thought dunderhead my given name."

"*I challenge you to beat me,*" he went on. "*First time, you win a half pound. After that, you beat me for the fun of it. I'm not the world's best chess player, yet it may take you some time.*"

"It took some time. Most a the school year. In two years, Mister Fisher taught me far more than chess. Taught me all my father couldn't teach. He filled this empty vessel. I was able ta turn Davy 'round as well, till he's near my match at chess. He's become a fine smith with no ounce a Dad's poor temper.

"Next summer me an' Davy enjoyed studying a crossbow Dad took in trade. We fashioned hundreds a arrows. Target-fired 'em in the back forest so much we put a stout tree down. Most fortunately it didn't land on us. 'Twas all ta satisfy our curiosity on what might give an arrow its best accuracy.

"The next year I grew near a foot. Dad deemed me size an' age ta take on smithing. Davy came ta the shop a year later. Good, quick students, we changed his disposition toward us. 'Twas there, in our spare time, we applied what we'd learned on arrows ta cannonballs. Fashioned those strangely shaped ones so dead accurate. We found some new cannon ideas as well, yet 'twas mostly the balls' shape that gave 'em their fine accuracy. Still smithing, 'tis Davy who's kept us supplied with our magical dead-aiming balls on the *Vengeferth*.

"So 'twas, men. Those magical guns were made by us Werthman brothers, Davy an' me. An' more a the magic was in the balls' funny shape. Now, I beg ya agree that those secrets a our magical guns must go unmentioned beyond these walls at least for a time. I've no plan ta go back pirating, an' I wish the details a those guns ta go ta the grave with Davy an' me. I'll not improve this world's war machines. 'Tis no legacy I'd consider. When I see 'im soon, I'm sure Davy'll agree.

"Ya know little a the guns or balls, men. Yet their mention might bring war mongers searching me out ta pester. The guns'r far known, yet in a storied way. Let's leave 'em there."

After a short pause in silence, I cleared my throat. My gaze'd been awhile on dreamy eyed Doc, smiling an' nodding his head.

"Captain," I stated. "I believe four crewmen here should learn that the man seated by ya is a the name Doc Fisher."

Reed, Gorden, Dessinger, an' Heitman turned ta laughing an' chirping, till Gorden asked out, "Captain, how the devil'd the two a ya find your way a' sea aboard the *Vengeferth?*"

"Back then the famine drove a number a good men out, yet 'tis a lengthy story," Captain Werthman sighed, "an' I've gone on long. We'll hold that tale for another eve."

"But Captain," Gorden put in, "another eve mightn't come around in this lifetime if we soon travel our own ways."

We glanced about, viewing the dear friends in life we'd found our closest comfort with. Seemed true that we'd so soon part ways. It turned to a sadly clumsy moment begging another pint a ale, even two. Yet there an' then we hatched our plan.

We jawed on it, an' clearly the idea a the *Vengeferth* crew going down with the ship wouldn't float. A flock out there knew the lie in it, so the story'd get out. Even should the flock be quiet as church mice, we seven enjoyed warm pubs. Which a us, jaw oiled by spirits, could keep from filling the room with such a wondrous tale? Myself stood likely ta be first guilty.

Also, 'twas pointed out, we may lose ourselves in the crowd, but there were seafarers, scattered afar, pining for shiny trinkets or lost fingers. They might show any day, with a keen eye, an' clearly recall any a our handsome faces an' kindly voices.

Yet our Captain had ta waken with another large problem daily. 'Twas his far known de Bergerac proboscis. It could find no way ta disguise itself. He *might* hide it in the back a his own small smithing shop, quietly keeping his nose ta the grindstone, so ta speak, but all knew 'twas not his true nature.

That night our plan was struck. We'd travel ta the colonies where a man's past was past. Many went there for start overs. Any but the most grievous mistakes went forgave an' forgot.

Captain paid the passage for us all ta the new world. Seems he had some rich money an' fine trinkets in his brother's keeping. Doc an' me had set by our tidy sums a money an' some trinkets, but the Captain's cache 'twas a true pirate's treasure.

Though none but Reed had the least desire ta reset a foot aboard any sea going vessel, the promise a us having new beginnings together won the day. A month on we booked passage. Then we all much enjoyed a fine, uneventfull trip.

(53) The stuff since

Our last voyage is some years behind us. 'Tis a tale far more enjoyed in the telling than 'twas in living through. It took months from our lives, yet seemed years.

Here in Boston, Captain Werthman an' Gorden own a fine smithing shop. Doc lives above his doctoring office across the street. I'm the upper flat neighbor next ta Doc. Werthman an' Gorden married lovely sisters an' now Doc's married 'imself a fine wife as well. I've oft said I'm a bit old for all that, yet a late I made friends with a nice widow.

Gorden's hair's more moderate ta the style. Took up the chess game last year till I can no longer best 'im. Eight in ten he thumps Doc or Captain Werthman as well. Reed's first mate on a freighter out a New York. Sports a fine red beard, an' locks ta the shoulder as Gorden had. Last year he delivered news that Reverend Jo an' his flock took up the fight against slavery.

Espying Heitman an' Dessinger's faces drawn on posters last week, I went out ta see 'em. Hadn't jawed with the two in a time. Timmons Meadow was all set up, jugglers an' jesters wandering about, an' the gamesters at tables taking your farthings. 'Twas a noisy, milling crowd, many in their Sunday best. In the middle two poles stood with a line across.

Soon horns sounded above the noise. The crowd hushed, eyes went up, an' there were Dessinger an' Heitman each clambering up a pole. Appeared near twenty five foot up, an seemed a fall'd be life threatening. They walked about up there just fine. Seemed as easy as working the *Vengeferth's* riggin. Yet once their rope wavered an' we gasped. Most fortunately neither fell.

Back a' ground, the two soon heard my voice in the crowd, an' hurried o'er, happy ta greet me, shaking my hand.

"So, Mister Devoe, how ya be? Are the others well? D' ya like our show up there?" they asked, smiling, an' laughing about.

"I'm fine, as are the rest. Ya look at ease up there, like 'tis the *Vengeferth's* riggin. Yet your misstep did take my breath."

"'Tis easier 'n the riggin, Mister DeVoe," Heitman chuckled. "Easy as a biscuit. No chop under, moving the line. A' times we jiggle the line a tad, just ta keep us all from dozing off."

We jawed, an' I gave 'em news a the others. Doc had wed since they were by, an' Gorden's wife was with a first child.

Slapping the reigns lightly, I turned the horses home. Shook my head laughing. Imagine the young pips giving me half a heart attack jiggling the line a time ta keep us awake. Well, in our youth, I suppose we all jiggle the line a time or two ta keep us awake. I'm ta the age where I'd more thank ya for the nap.

THE END
* * *

*Aye, we seven lived a fierce adventure. Good Captain Werthman found a worthy notion, an' it seems my most weary hand wielded a passable pen. Fine friend Doc made time ta edit as well. Yet this stellar tale needs **your** aid ta complete its life. Ya can help it escape the heart a Amazon's darkest shelves ta the sunlight it deserves.*

*As surely as Captain charged me with putting the story ta the page, **I now charge ya** with gifting for'rd a small few a its copies ta friends young or old. Consider yourself thus charged **only** should ya deem it a sparkling pirate treasure well worthy a recommendation. You're the tale's best good hope, as your friends may gift it ta their friends.*

I reveal in strictest confidence, H44ANSMZ, known this year ta save a buck deep in the Amazon,. This pirate code secretly says **I'm Wil DeVoe's Friend**. *'Twill be no fib, as I feel we struck some friendship as your fingers walked the pages.*

G'day, an' a most humble an' hearty thanks ta ya,
Wil DeVoe

Editor Doc, (again pesty) insists I translate this from "piratese."

If you found *Last Voyage a the Vengeferth* a fine treasure, please gift it to some dear friends or relatives, perhaps at birthday or Christmas. (Best gift ideas oft being a hard find.) You'll help this tale gift its pleasure to the world. You're its best good chance. H44ANSMZ is a code you may use at Amazon to save a dollar on each copy. (Yet hurry. 'Twill one day go lost on the Amazon.)

Thank you, Will (Aka Greg Schindler) DeVoe

Writer's blog:

I hatched the idea for this book in December of 2015. Five months along, the story was 90% whole. I spent the summer months gardening whilst it percolated in my mind's recesses. I counted it complete the next December. Then came months of editing and revision, with the addition of two more chapters (52 and finally 20).

The tale got its start from the boy-in-the-chair scene, which I'm told was an authentic pirate activity, unlike walking the plank.

During the writing and editing I found myself oft thinking in "piratese". A' times it crept into my speech, and still does. Might I be permanently afflicted?

In editing the language, I struggled to balance "truthiness" and readability. I hope you found it a pleasurable, palatable balance.

My hope is that the book gave you as much fun in the reading as it gave me in its creation. Yet the advantage is to me, as I enjoyed hundreds of hours. But don't tell the wife. She insists 'twas work.

Reviews on Amazon are coveted and *most* appreciated. It's another way ya might help the book gift its pleasure to the world.

I invite ya to read *Shrugg, 1 Mile*. 'Tis so different, yet I *guarantee* every ounce a good tale. An easier read, yet be warned, should ya hurry along, y'll miss the huge, tiny clue early, then slap yourself upside the head when 'tis pointed out later along.

Website <http://www.g-a-schindlerauthorpage.com>
Email <gregsdaylily@hotmail.com>

Other books on Amazon by G. A. Schindler:

Shrugg, 1 Mile--science fiction novella (I rate it PG15).

Footprints--three parts: poetry, songs & humor.

Love is the Smile--an adult book about love in long term relationships. (R rated)

Great Speckled Banana's Great Quest--a humorous book for children from 3 to 103."

Timmy and the Hotdog Song--another funny children's book. It was chosen for the public schools' national "Ask Twice" program.

I'll Solve the Crime, Justin Tyme--yet another humorous children's book.

Made in the USA
Columbia, SC
23 December 2017